Praise for ASSASSINS & OLYMPIANS

"Marie Howalt's *Assassins & Olympians* is a joy to read, a very clever sci-fi detective novel wrapped around a reflection on violence and trust. Funny and smart, it is a page-turner that all lovers of original universes will undoubtedly appreciate. Very highly recommended."

— Seb Doubinsky, author of *Missing Signal*, *The Invisible*, and *Paperclip*

"A slick, funny blend of noir detective story and sci-fi adventure, *Assassins & Olympians* is a spacey romp. Howalt has a flair for snappy dialogue (grumpy pilot Eddie is a particular treat) and the world-building is admirably light-touch, utilising nuggets of information from dispatches, instructions, news reports, and even excerpts from interstellar detective series Worra & Darith. A quick, entertaining read, *Assassins & Olympians* leaves the reader wanting more cases from (and more background information on) the quirky staff of Colibri Investigations. A winning and well-crafted universe."

— Tracy Fahey, author of *I Spit Myself Out* and *The Unheimlich Manoeuvre*

"*Assassins & Olympians* is a right romp, filled with energetic characters in a galaxy that breathes, and a worthy sequel to its predecessor. I'm a little terrified of Howalt's ability to write characters..."

— Aden Ng, author of *Tearha*

"Prepare to be blown away by exceptional world-building, and a cast of characters you can't help but fall in love with. [In *Assassins & Olympians*], Eddie, Richard, and Alannah are back at it in the best possible way. This is a must-read sci-fi gem, with a diverse cast and an intriguing world. If you love sci-fi from authors like Douglas Adams or John Scalzi, you'll adore this."

— Kathy Joy, author of *Last One to the Bridge*

"Fun private-eye mystery in a sci-fi setting with casual inclusivity, found family, and multiple worlds. Reminiscent of Kristine Kathryn Rusch and NL Haverstock."

— Si Clarke, author of *The Left Hand of Dog*

"In this riveting science fiction adventure, [Marie Howalt] masterfully blends elements of action, mystery, and futuristic alien technology for a plot that is fast-paced and pulse-pounding. I loved this interstellar adventure! [The author} did an amazing job of crafting a fun, quirky adventure. *Assassins & Olympians* is a must read for fans of the space opera sci-fi style genre."

— Paige Lovitt, *Reader Views*

COLIBRI INVESTIGATIONS

ASSASSINS & OLYMPIANS

MARIE HOWALT

Denver, Colorado

Published in the United States by:
Spaceboy Books LLC
1627 Vine Street
Denver, CO 80206
www.readspaceboy.com

Cover art includes CC0 art via Pixabay

ISBN: 978-1-951393-25-0
First printed September 2023

For Jonna
who sparked my interest in the English language and its literature

Dwebl's cities are constructed much like their counterparts on the zetoi homeworld Ahlm, with an affinity for sky high buildings, and a layout that reflects social status in a vertical manner.

That is to say, the wealthier and healthier the person, the higher up you will find the home they live in. And although lower entrances, stairs, elevators and escalators have become the norm to accommodate zetois with disabilities as well as the needs of other species who can't fly, you will still come across the more traditional dwellings in the upper class neighborhoods. You may also notice a tendency toward a distribution of the less fortunate in the parts of the cityscape with more ground-level housings.

If this kind of demographic division offends you, as a person or as a species, you may find solace in the fact that crime rates are generally very low in zetoi settlements and on their stations. Though perhaps this is not only a testament to a functioning public welfare system but also to the zetois' strict weapon regulations. Be sure to leave any pocket knives or defense shockers behind before attempting to enter a zetoi community. Allegedly, even military personnel of other species have trouble convincing the local authorities of their right to or need for dart guns even with non-lethal darts.

— Alannah Jackson, *Interstellar Sightseeing 101*

1

BUSINESS AS USUAL

"Nosy feather dusters," Eddie muttered.

At least, Richard hoped he was right that she only muttered it. Sometimes, his auditory verbal agnosia made the distinction between a mumble and clearly spoken sentences a bit difficult. But no one was looking closely at the pair of humans as they made their way out of Dwebl's primary chick— no, *shuttle* port. Dammit.

"Eddie," Richard said in the tone he used when he really wanted to issue an order but couldn't quite justify it. "That is both specieist and completely uncalled for. They were only doing their job." Though, Eddie wasn't actually a specieist. She was just an asshole sometimes. To everybody regardless of species. "And besides, I'm not sure calling someone with a beak nosy makes sense," he added as an afterthought.

Richard stole a brief glance at his patch and then made a gesture for his pilot to turn down a, thankfully, less crowded street.

Eddie replied something he didn't catch, and Richard decided to ignore it. Sure, he had rough edges, but he'd been through the Terran Defense Force diplomacy mill in his former line of work and knew better than to insult possibly the most influential species in their category of the galactic Union.

Still, he did share her unease about the procedure in the shuttle port. Sometimes the subjects of *Colibri* Investigations' scrutiny turned hostile, and Richard vastly preferred being armed to back up his incentives for cooperation. As it were, the zetoi authorities had balked at this and confiscated most of his and Eddie's arsenal, only allowing them to keep one single dart gun with fairly harmless darts between them. And it was only Richard's convincing weapon licenses and registration as a private investigator that had let them get away with that much. Well, perhaps his appearance had helped convey the right message too. Richard looked like a law-abiding citizen, tall enough to look the zetois in the eye and wearing a sober outfit in a faintly army-inspired cut. He had neatly trimmed short, black hair greying at the temples in what Richard himself liked to think of as a distinguished sort of way and only a fashionable amount of scruff on his face.

Eddie had managed to convince the zetois that the cable strips in her pocket were for equipment maintenance by blurting out some technobabble about what spaceship pilots used those for.

Richard stopped and took in their surroundings. All around them, the city sprawled upward, the evening sky above almost entirely obscured from this angle by the higher streets and bright lights. Down here, everything was a bit murky. It would be the most logical place for someone from off-world to hide. Like every other big city in the galaxy's myriad of planets, Naiwon had inhabitants and tourists of several species, although the original settlers were always the predominant species. "All right," he said.

"Split up and look for the fucker?" Eddie suggested. She wasn't uncouth, but she liked, Richard thought, to project toughness, and she did it well. Eddie was, as always, wearing tight, black pants, a loose top under her signature battered, old ecoleather jacket, and a slightly sardonic expression. Her dark hair would be practical if not for the fact that the front part tended to be just long enough to fall into her eyes.

"Can we agree to call the person we are looking for our target?" Richard sighed with very little hope of revolutionizing his pilot's selective vocabulary. "But yes. Let's split up. Ask around. Look for signs of human inhabitants that match our target's features. But don't attempt to apprehend him on your own."

"Why? Someone who does insurance fraud doesn't sound like a dangerous person," Eddie said, scanning the street with her gaze. It forked up ahead.

"Nevertheless. We can't know how desperate he is. And," Richard added, changing tactics, "you aren't licensed to take him here. I don't want any trouble with the local authorities." The local authorities who had not only confiscated their weapons but also told them there was no record of a person by the name they were searching for anywhere on Dwebl.

Eddie nodded. "Left or right?"

"You go left. Notify me if you find anything or anyone of interest. And here. Take this." Richard pulled out his dart gun from its holster under his jacket. "And stop arguing."

"I didn't say anything!" Eddie huffed.

"You were thinking it," Richard said, waving the gun at her. It was an old argument. Eddie thought she was good in a fight, and she was. Especially when her reflexes were scarily keen from hyper. But her last dose had worn off several hours ago at this point. Anyway, she might do well in a bar brawl, but Richard was military trained. And there was a difference regardless of what she was inclined to think.

Eddie rolled her eyes and snatched the weapon from him. "Don't blame me if a zetoi comes flying at you and mugs you."

"Highly unlikely," he returned.

Eddie put the dart gun out of sight inside her own jacket, and gave him a two-fingered salute that had nothing to do with discipline. She headed left.

Richard rolled his shoulders and went right. From Alannah's intel... Okay, from Alannah's tourist guide notes and presentation the previous day in the *Colibri*'s galley, he knew that he was headed into a decidedly more decrepit neighborhood than Eddie. The street sloped downward as if to make a point about social status. There were street lights, but they were few and far between. A zetoi was standing at a corner, the feathers crowning her head dull and matted. She looked at him furtively.

Of all the category 3 species in the galaxy, the zetois were Richard's least favorite to deal with in person. And that had nothing to do with their weapon restrictions. Their physiology was the main problem. Calling zetois birds was more inaccurate than calling humans monkeys. From an evolutionary standpoint, they were far removed from their avian ancestors, but there were similarities. Still, it was not that Richard minded people with feathers instead of hair or scales or had anything against arms that doubled as wings when stretched out and used for flight. He also did not feel particularly threatened by people whose fingers had sharp talons or made the average human lifespan seem like a fleeting moment. No, it was the fact that talking to people who had a beak instead of a mouth was nearly impossible when you relied on lipreading.

Richard set his patch to voice recognition. "Hello," he said in Standard. "Do you happen to know if there are any humans living nearby?"

The zetoi replied. In Standard, but not very forthcomingly Richard discovered when he read the transcription.

"I'm looking for a friend who went to Naiwon a month ago," Richard expanded. "It would be a great help to know if there are any human communities around here."

She clacked her bill in the zetoi negative. "Haven't seen any mammals lately," the transcription read.

"All right. Thank you for your time. May I send you my contact info in case you think of something? I can compensate you for the trouble," he added.

The zetoi held up her feathered forearm. No patch. That was uncommon and almost unheard of in human settlements. Well, he had come prepared for every eventuality. Richard reached into his jacket, ignored the zetoi's flinch and pulled out a business card that could be scanned on any patch or public terminal.

She took it without great enthusiasm.

This place reminded Richard of how he met Eddie. It had the same air of quiet hostility. The same smell of... poverty was the best word he could think of. He moved on down the street.

After a few minutes, Richard was starting to think the search would prove fruitless in this direction. Above him, traffic moved by, but on this level, the street was getting increasingly more derelict and deserted. He ducked in between two buildings only to discover it was a dead end. The houses met in front of him and had no doors or windows on this side.

Quick, soft footsteps approached him from behind. Richard snapped to attention. He had not seen anyone in the street before going into this cul-de-sac. And the footsteps were too quiet and too deliberate to be good news. Especially in a place like this. This was someone following him and hoping he didn't notice. Richard twisted out of the way, turning to face his assailant at the last possible moment and brought up his elbow to land a quick, precise blow.

The other person did take one step back, but that was all. No cry of pain, no falling. And not because Richard had misjudged; his elbow had connected precisely as intended. Richard stepped back, assessing his attacker. Despite being human, the person did not resemble Richard's target even remotely. This was a young, white man with a strawberry blond stubble of hair on his head. He was dressed in black, but had done nothing to disguise his facial features which probably meant he was here for the kill. His eyes were a startlingly clear blue color, one of them brimming with tears from the blow. He did nothing to wipe them away. He did nothing to mop away the blood slobbering down his face from his broken nose, either.

"I'll take an apology now," Richard said. He would. He would let the kid, because this guy could not possibly be more than 20 or 25 at the most, walk away to nurse his now slightly less handsome face. He might have picked Richard for an easy target. Might have followed him and Eddie, waited until they split up and taken him for the easier or the wealthier victim.

Oh, who was he kidding? Richard knew the moment their eyes met that this wasn't the kind of random mugging Eddie had talked about. He even felt oddly certain that this had nothing at all to do with their current case.

The assailant went in for the next attack instead of replying. Good form, too. Richard blocked the punch, but barely. His own counterattack was deflected with disturbing ease. The kid wasn't drawing a weapon. He probably had been stripped by the local authorities, too. And he had not bothered to find a discarded metal pipe or piece of concrete anywhere to hit Richard with, so he clearly expected to be able to take out a bigger, heavier person without a hitch.

The next punch Richard managed to land did not work like it should. Richard was usually pretty efficient in hand-to-hand combat, so he was surprised to see the young man barely sway at the blow that should by all reasonable standards have knocked him off his feet.

This whole situation was quickly turning into the proverbial collision with a supernova. Richard touched his patch in a quick pattern, a pre-arranged emergency code to alert Eddie of his location.

It was not until they were grappling on the grimy ground and his attacker grabbed his throat that Richard realized what the problem was. He attempted to pry away the fingers, tried to twist the wrist, but what he felt underneath the young man's glove and sleeve was not skin and flesh. It was unyielding metal.

Lots of people had prosthetics, of course. Usually they did not forgo synthetic flesh, but some probably did. The artificial hand paired with the fact that this young man fought in a way that made military officers appear sloppy, though... Damn. This had to be an enhanced soldier. But why? Why was Richard being attacked by an enhanced?

Somehow, he managed to punch the enhanced in the mouth, blood spraying right back into his own face. That, at least, made the would-be killer loosen his grip enough for Richard to strike at his elbow joints. They rolled, got to their feet. Richard had fought some badass fistfighters in his early military days, but he had never seen anyone completely disregard their injuries like this guy. Humans were programmed to react to damages done to their faces. Humans— The enhanced punched Richard so hard that he doubled over, heaving for breath and in danger of spilling his lunch. Now, as inconvenient as that was, it was how humans were supposed to react. And why was Eddie not here yet? It should not take her this long to get here. Hadn't he got the signal right? There was no time to check his patch now.

The enhanced pushed him back, and Richard stumbled into the solid wall of the closest building. The attacker had him by the throat again in a second and squeezed. Richard clawed at him, but it was futile. He kicked, and that was useless too. And the metal hand was choking him so efficiently that he was already starting to black out.

Then there was movement, the hand around his throat spasmed and let go, and Richard fell to his knees, gasping, coughing, waiting for his vision to clear.

Someone was shouting. When he looked up, the enhanced was on his knees, trying to get back to his feet. Eddie fired one more dart at his chest at point blank. And another. Finally, the young man fell back motionless on the ground.

Eddie exclaimed something that was probably shit, fuck, or a similar profanity. She stepped back and turned to Richard. "Are you okay?"

"I'm fine," Richard said. And turned away to throw up.

"Sorry for the wait," she said when he was done retching. She had rolled the enhanced over and was tying his hands behind his back with her cable strips. "I had to shoot him twice before he even reacted. And then twice more."

Richard waved the apology away. "He's an enhanced," he said. His throat felt bruised and raw.

Eddie pursed her lips. "That... explains a lot... Except why he attacked you."

"We'll have to wait until he wakes up to find out," Richard said and spat out the last bile in his mouth. "Let's get him back to the ship."

"I'm sorry, it sounded like you said we should take him back to the *Colibri*," Eddie said.

"I did. We can't just leave him here."

Eddie made an aborting gesture. "Yes, we can! He tried to kill you!"

Richard held up a hand. "That is exactly why we should take him back with us. I want to know why. I don't think this has anything to do with our case. I want to know who wants me dead."

Eddie prodded the limp body on the ground with her foot. Under other circumstances, Richard would have objected, but he would let this one pass. "But my girl," Eddie said.

"Alannah will be fine," Richard smirked despite the situation.

"The *Colibri*, you ass," Eddie told him.

"Will also be fine. The ship as well as my ass." Richard touched his neck. He would sport quite a bruise later, though.

"But how are you even going to get him past the authorities?"

Richard looked down at the unconscious kid. "You mean the guy who staged his own death and ran away with the insurance money, which is strictly a human problem and none of the zetoi authorities' concern?"

"He doesn't even look like the guy!" Eddie argued.

"Well," Richard said, "They don't know that."

Welcome to the assisted tour of this passer class ship's medbay facilities. Please point your patch's camera to any piece of equipment for an explanation of its use.

Examination table/recuperation cot.

In order to save precious space on board small vessels, the CareLab ExamRecup system easily converts from examination table to recuperation cot and back again, allowing you to make the best of the allotted space. Instructions are located next to the conversion switch. Please do not attempt conversion while occupied.

Pharmaceutical storage unit.

In this cabinet, you will find medication, first-aid materials and non-prescription health aids such as pain relievers, wound sealants, anti-nausea sprays, disinfectants, quickcasts, etc. If a red light is blinking next to one of the shelves, one of the products is missing or past its expiration date.

Please note: CareLab is not responsible for the contents of this unit or any misuse of them. The contents are intended for human use and may not be suitable for other species.

MedPal.2.

Using innovative technology from CareLab, MedPal.2 is the ultimate personal health assistant for a modern medbay where healthcare professionals are not a viable option. Place MedPal.2's scanner next to the patient's area of complaint, select scan in the menu and wait for the indicator on the left side of the display to turn green. It normally only takes MedPal.2 60 to 180 seconds to determine the cause of the complaint. Treatment suggestions with detailed walkthroughs will be available as text or audio. Often, MedPal.2 will be able to perform treatment of superficial injuries as well as simple surgery, such as removal of shrapnel or foreign objects in non-critical areas of the body.

Please note: In case of serious illness or injury, it is always best to consult a professional doctor or nurse. The equipment is intended for diagnosis and treatment of humans and may not be suitable for other species.

Safety equipment cabinet.

Inside, you will find CareLab's BioSafeKit, an assortment of sterile equipment such as courtesy masks, neonitril gloves and a pelso coated jumpsuit to keep you safe in case of high radiation values, viruses or other contaminants. All items come with instruction manuals to assure safe use.

Thank you for choosing CareLab! We strive to minimize your health issues and unit issues at the same time by providing high grade medical equipment at a low cost. Please consult our catalog for a complete list of our available services and equipment and don't hesitate to contact us if you have any questions.

— CareLab's interactive medbay guide

2

ENHANCED COMPLICATIONS

The *Colibri* never spoke. For the first couple of weeks on board the small ship, Alannah had found it slightly off-putting. As a norm, everything gave verbal reports. Patches, air conditioners, 3D printers, fridges and, of course, spaceships. There were speakers everywhere in raphinae and laridae class ships, and even on the few privately owned vessels she had traveled on, Alannah had been informed of approaches to stations, delays, and countdowns to hyperjumps by the ship's computer. But the *Colibri* was silent. Alannah would get written messages on her patch instead. It made sense, of course. She couldn't imagine what it must be like for Richard to hear the noise but not understand a word when someone spoke.

The ship did use non-verbal sounds in addition to messages written out on screens, however, and a quiet chirp from a speaker made Alannah look up from the article she was working on. That signal meant the chick had returned from its trip to Dwebl.

She blinked and pushed back a few pastel purple strands of curly hair that had spilled from the messy bun on her head, a contrast to the yellow patterned shirt she was wearing today. Wasn't it early for the the others to return? She wasn't sure. This was only Richard and Eddie's third job since Alannah was hired as their live-in consultant, so she didn't know much about the routines of various job types. Still, accounting for the time it usually took to get through zetoi security, they must have been extremely efficient if they had already located the person they were hired to find and made it back to the ship again. Letting her curiosity win, Alannah left her writing and made her way through the ship to the nest. Although some people might think of her as the odd one out compared to her two taller, less approachable looking and largely monochromatically dressed companions, she had quickly begun to feel right at home on the little spaceship. She really had the sense that she was part of the crew now.

The *Colibri* was a passer class ship, small by definition and not particularly luxurious. But she had more than enough room for three people as long as they didn't mind sharing a kitchen and a bathroom. She was kept in good repair and had a great artificial gravity system and sufficiently dense pelso plating on the outer hull to keep everyone inside safe.

Alannah clearly arrived in time for the nest to have repressurized because the door sealing it off from the rest of the *Colibri* was sliding open.

Alannah smiled as Eddie came through. "Hi," she said, "How was the—"

Eddie did not look happy. In fact, she looked more disgruntled than Alannah had ever seen her, and that was saying something since disgruntled was one of her basic settings. "There were some complications," Eddie growled. Then, maybe remembering her manners, forced a smile. "Hi, Alannah."

"Compli—" was as far as Alannah got this time.

Richard appeared behind Eddie. His face looked like someone had given it a solid punch or two, and there were flecks of dried blood on it as well. He had something... No, Alannah realized, he had someone slung over his shoulder.

"I— Um, is that person related to those complications?" Alannah squeaked. She mentally rewound. *Colibri* Investigations had been supposed to find someone who had staged his own death and run away from human space with the money from his life insurance. Was this how they usually brought in their targets?

"Yep," Eddie said without looking back at Richard. "He insisted."

"Alannah," Richard said, his voice a bit strained under the weight of the other person. Or body. Hopefully person. "We have a guest."

She studied his burden as Richard marched past her. Her mouth fell open. "But that isn't the person you were looking for. Is it?" Sure, cosmetic surgery could do a great deal, and he might have started an efficient workout routine during his career as a runaway, but Alannah was pretty sure this person was way too young. "Is this guest dead or alive?" she asked.

"He's just unconscious," Eddie said, falling into step with Alannah behind Richard. "And we didn't have time to locate our real target before that guy located us."

"But who is he?" Alannah asked.

"We don't know. He attacked Richard and I got him with a dart gun. Richard thinks he's a hitman and insisted on bringing him here to find out who hired him."

"But... How did you even get him past zetoi authorities?" Alannah asked.

Eddie shrugged. "We told them he was the guy we'd come looking for. That he attacked us and we had to temporarily neutralize him."

"But!" Alannah said again. There was too much relevant stuff to put after that word, and she didn't know where to begin.

"You know the zetoi. We all look the same to them. And they were just happy to get rid of an unregistered human on their planet."

"Eddie!" Richard called. "We need to secure him in medbay before he wakes up again."

Alannah studied the unconscious would-be killer. His pale face looked agonizingly young. Someone, Richard or Eddie presumably, had clearly broken his nose, and his face was splattered with blood. His hands were tied and hung limply down Richard's back.

"He's just a boy," Alannah breathed.

"Not really," Eddie said. "He's an enhanced."

Alannah gaped. "Come again? An enhanced?"

"It was Richard's idea," Eddie said, which seemed to be her go-to explanation today. "I told him it's a bad idea to bring that guy on board."

"I don't know what you are saying, Eddie," called Richard from a few paces ahead of them, "but I can tell you are saying it with ill-concealed contempt."

None of them replied. It wasn't like he would be able to understand their retort anyway.

They reached medbay, and Richard unceremoniously dumped the enhanced on the cot. And that was the moment he regained consciousness.

"Shit!" Eddie exclaimed as the young man sat bolt upright.

Richard immediately tried to push him back, but Alannah could tell he stood no chance of holding the enhanced down, even if his hands were tied.

Eddie dropped the bags on Alannah's feet, which she wasn't going to hold against her right now, and drew her dart gun. As Alannah watched, Richard struggled with the young man, and Eddie jammed the barrel of the gun into his chest and pressed the trigger. For an uncomfortable moment, the young man kept fighting. He looked helpless now, hurt and barely more than a teenager.

"Restraints!" Richard barked when finally the enhanced lay motionless on the cot again.

Alannah was usually good under pressure, but she found herself staring as Eddie pulled open a drawer and fished out what looked like extremely tough belts. Why did they even have those?

15

"Phew," Richard said, standing back after tying down the unconscious boy. They had placed restraints around his waist and legs and both arms instead of the cable strips.

"Are you okay?" Eddie asked Alannah.

"Am I—" Alannah shook her head in disbelief. "What is wrong with you two?"

"Wrong?" Richard repeated. "What do you mean?" Now that Alannah looked at him more closely, she could see the beginning of bruising around his neck too.

"I mean," she began, "that you just abducted a kid, beat him up, shot him with a dart gun, several times, and tied him up, and you are completely unfazed about the whole thing!"

"He's not a kid," Eddie said. "He's an enhanced soldier who tried to kill Richard."

"Which does not make it better!" Alannah shouted. "You brought an assassin with superhuman strength on board the *Colibri*! Are you idiots? No, don't answer," she added. "Give me a bowl of water and a rag."

They both stared at her like she had sprouted two heads. "Hello? I know you can process speech," she told Eddie, "and I saw you read my lips," she added to Richard.

"What for?" Richard asked.

"Well, someone clearly broke his nose," Alannah said slowly, pointing at the unconscious kid. "I am going to clean up his face. I'm sure you can clean up yourself, Richard."

"I thought you hated the idea of us bringing him on board," Eddie argued.

"I do!" Alannah planted her hands on her hips and glared at them both. "But now that he is here, I also insist that we treat him humanely."

At least they had the decency to look ever so slightly abashed. Richard began to rummage around for the items she had asked for.

Alannah took the bowl and rag that he managed to produce and bent over the prisoner. The idiots may call him a guest, but that was obviously the euphemism of the year.

She carefully wiped blood away from his lips and chin. Some of it was dry already, but as she approached his nose, there was fresh blood too. The water in the bowl quickly grew pink. She studied him more closely. There was a crisscrossing pattern of scars around his left eye that made Alannah wonder if he had an ocular implant. Without half his face covered in blood and snot, he was a pretty boy, really.

"Alannah."

She turned to Richard. He had mopped blood off his own face now.

"Enhanced soldiers are full of nanobots."

Alannah almost told him that he was full of something else, but opted for gesturing for him to go on instead.

"They weren't only created for faster reflexes and strength. He will heal quickly."

Telling him that was hardly an excuse to beat up a kid did cross Alannah's mind. But... when did she get this protective? She didn't know the boy. And, more importantly, he had tried to kill Richard. Had most likely killed before, as a soldier or an assassin, or both. She realized two things. First of all, she was not able to withstand seeing someone being manhandled, shot, and tied down right in front of her without automatically feeling sorry for them. And secondly, she had an annoying weakness for lost causes. Just look at exhibit A and B right here next to her. "Good," she said. "So what now?"

"Now we wait for him to wake up," Richard said. He turned his back on her and Eddie and retrieved a couple of tablets and a bottle of water from a cabinet. "Unlike him, I don't bounce back with inhuman speed," he added after swallowing the pain killers.

"You are also a lot older," Eddie said.

"And when he wakes up," Alannah cut through what was probably going to be the beginning of their habitual bickering, "what then?"

"Then I question him," Richard said.

"What does that mean?" Alannah asked. "Look, I just want to know if I'm going to have to watch you torture a kid."

There was the briefest of pauses before Richard replied. Despite his words, Alannah did not like that pause. "I am not going to torture him, Alannah. I am going to ask him some questions."

"And if he won't answer?"

"I need to know why he tried to kill me. I need to know who wants me dead. If it has anything to do with the insurance fraud case or something else entirely. If I'm the only one in danger, or if Eddie is too. I'm not asking you to stay here while I do that."

Their eyes locked for a moment. Alannah was trying to gauge how far Richard would go to get those answers. "I'll stay," she said.

Eddie swiveled around a chair and sat on it with her arms on the backrest. "The more the merrier," she said, not merrily at all.

VoidSearch: *enhanced*
>   Results:
>>   *enhanced skin in three easy steps (sponsored ad)*
>>   *enhanced performance in bed*
>>   *how to get enhanced results from investment*
>>   *enhance your sex life with this ancient wendek trick*

VoidSearch: *enhanced+soldier*
>   Results:
>>   *sexy cyborg: confessions of an enhanced soldier*
>>   *warfare as an aphrodisiac enhancement: why draever soldiers can keep going all night*
>>   *dirty soldier dreams on X-tream*

VoidSearch: *enhanced+soldier+tdf-(x-tream,sex)*
>   Results:
>>   *What was the enhanced program, and why did the Terran Defense Force abandon it?*
>>   *Dark Secrets of the TDF*
>>   *The aliens hate us, and here is why*

Selected:
>>   *What was the enhanced program, and why did the Terran Defense Force abandon it?*

When humanity discovered that not only is the galaxy teeming with intelligent life, but also home of a Union of species spanning a large number of solar systems, we furthermore discovered that several of these species are more technologically advanced than anything humans can boast. In addition to this, many also have physical and mental abilities that we are simply incapable of matching. In other words, we found ourselves further down the food chain than we liked.

The Union does not expect or order its members to dismantle their own military forces. Just take the draevere as an example; much of their interstellar presence is based on a military structure. And so, the Terran Defense Force itself is not in violation of any treaties. It even has staff stationed in systems dominated by other species.

The idea of the enhanced soldier program was claimed to be an attempt at matching the abilities of some of our fellow species, though that may not be the whole truth. The concept was simple enough: Recruit volunteers to have a number of improvements, or enhancements if you will, done in order to make them better soldiers. Among these were neural implants that dampen pain, an internal chronometer, dark vision and a host of nanobots that speed up the healing process in case of injury. The list here is inconclusive, but that is due to the classified nature of the program. It is very nearly impossible to find anyone willing to divulge specifics. What we do know is that the TDF also sought out volunteers among persons with prosthetic limbs so those could be replaced with state-of-the-art military grade parts. In short, the TDF attempted to create perfect, superhuman killing machines.

A number of the alterations done to the TDF's enhanced soldiers were in direct violation with interstellar conventions. Implants such as hearing aids or other helpful, medical disability compensations are, of course, perfectly accepted and legal, but attempting to artificially add abilities that are not a natural part of the human physique and mentality are not.

After a lengthy legal dispute, the TDF had to stop producing and using enhanced soldiers only a few years after the program was introduced.

— Article by Dalisay Fabroa, downloaded to Alannah Jackson's patch

3
BASIC INTERROGATION 101

Richard wasted no time waiting for the guest to wake up. He pulled off the enhanced assassin's gloves to reveal one artificial hand and one organic. The soldier's fingerprints matched nothing in the databases they had access to. Neither did his retina when Richard pried open the eyelid of his biological eye to scan it. He was wearing a patch, but it was a prime example of a typical burner with only a basic PlaNet connection and without the necessary identity verification to get a dispatch through VoidNet.

"Why are his prosthetics so..." Eddie made a vague gesture.

"Military grade," Richard explained while examining the inorganic hand. It was made of a solid gunmetal grey alloy. "They prioritize functionality over typical aesthetics. Especially with enhanced soldiers."

When the Force canceled the enhanced program, Richard had wondered what happened to the soldiers themselves. The news had been vague about it, saying they were dismissed from active service. But they were not meant to be sent back into civilian society with the modifications. Well, one of those soldiers still had his abilities and was putting them to use as a murderer, apparently.

Richard hoped that asking the ex-soldier nicely would do the trick. Alannah was adamantly opposed to forceful interrogation, and Richard would rather avoid it, too. Most of all because an enhanced soldier would be trained to withstand torture, so it would take more than chopping off a couple of fingers to make him talk.

The enhanced took a sudden, gasping breath. His eyes shot open, wide and unfocused for a few seconds. His artificial left eye reacted faster than its organic counterpart, though. He tried to sit, felt the restraints and jerked with more intent and force than was natural with the intense dart gun hangover he ought to have now. He tore at the restraints so hard that Richard was afraid he might actually break them.

"Stand down, soldier!" Richard barked in his most commanding officer's voice.

Miraculously, that made the enhanced freeze. The young man's gaze swept over the three of them in quick assessment of the situation, and then he slumped back on the cot.

"Thank you," Richard said, relieved. "What is your name?"

The young man's jaw was set. Now he stared resolutely at the ceiling.

"All right," Richard said, leaning into his line of sight. "You attempted to kill me, and you failed."

There was only a slight reaction at that. A tension of muscles around his mouth.

"You failed," Richard repeated, "and this is how it will go from here. I am going to ask you questions, and you will answer them."

The enhanced kept staring past Richard's face, his expression blank.

"You think you have an alternative," Richard continued, "and that is absolutely correct. You are currently on my spaceship. We are docked at Dwebl's space station. You are welcome not to answer my questions. Then I will simply contact the zetoi authorities and have a military unit escort you out of here. I am sure they will gladly hand you over to the Terran Defense Force. I assume the military would like to have you back, to punish you for any crimes you have committed after your discharge, and to dismantle you as you are no longer legal."

Now the young man was definitely reacting. He was doing a good job keeping still and looking neutrally bored, but his breathing had grown quicker.

"I'm a busy man, and you interrupted my work when you attacked me, so I don't want to waste my time on you. If you can't be bothered to answer, I'll arrange for your departure right away."

The enhanced soldier's pale lips were pressed tightly together.

"Understood," Richard said, straightening up, but making sure to keep an eye on the guest. "Eddie, will you let station security know we have a renegade human soldier in our custody and advise them to send an armed unit to take him away?"

"Wait."

Richard forced a smug smile from forming on his face. Eddie had not even managed an affirmation before the enhanced spoke.

Richard nodded. "All right, then. Let's start over, shall we? What is your name, soldier?"

The young man took a deep breath. "Kierran O'Connor," he said.

His expression was still controlled, but Richard saw the discomfort in his eyes. Or, well, eye. The artificial one didn't hold any emotion. But so far so good. Discomfort meant he was probably telling the truth. The inconvenient thing about that, of course, was that looking up his name was likely going to yield no information whatsoever. Had he managed to delete himself from all records? Or had the Force done that? Richard did not like the latter possibility one bit.

"All right, Kierran O'Connor," Richard said. "I am Captain Richard Hart, but I'm sure you know that. These are my associates, Eddie and Alannah." He nodded in their general direction, not taking his eyes off the enhanced's face.

Out of Richard's line of sight, someone made an exclamation. He could guess what it might be. A protest that he was giving away their names to the person who had attempted to kill him. But there was a point to this. Richard suspected that sometimes Eddie forgot he knew exactly what he was doing. Sure, she was smart and fast, and a great pilot. But she had no history in intelligence. Richard was working their guest as quickly as possible without resorting to cruelty or being too obvious about it. "I'm sure you know what I'm going to ask you."

The enhanced did not reply, of course. He knew better than answering anything that was not a direct question. That was basic interrogation 101.

Richard stepped around the recuperation cot to the other side. The enhanced did not watch him, but Richard wanted to add a bit of energy to this. It sometimes sped things up to suggest one was impatient and may resort to a number of methods. "Why did you try to kill me, Kierran O'Connor?"

"I was contracted," the enhanced replied, readily enough. It wasn't much of a revelation. Richard had known from the start the soldier wasn't after his money or organs or ship. He had also been pretty certain it was nothing personal.

"By whom?" Richard asked.

No reply.

Richard sighed, turned on his heel and strode purposefully towards the door. "Eddie, Alannah. Come on," he said as he passed them.

A protest from Eddie.

"Yes, we can," Richard replied, assuming she had objected to their leaving the enhanced alone. He turned to face their equally surprised expressions only after the door closed behind them.

"No, we can't!" Eddie was saying. "What if he breaks free?"

"He won't. Not in the next couple of minutes," Richard said in a hushed voice. The bulkheads were thick, but for all he knew, O'Connor's hearing may be as enhanced as the rest of him. "I want to give him a few moments to imagine how unpleasant it will be to be picked up by station security."

Alannah blinked, her mouth opening in comprehension.

"Oh, I'll go ahead and call them, then," Eddie said.

"No," Richard told her.

"No?" Eddie repeated. "What are you playing at?"

"The power of imagination," Richard replied with a wry smile.

"Funny," she hissed, "my imagination is great, and I can easily imagine an assassin with superhuman strength tearing apart the *Colibri*. I can imagine him pulling a kinetic gun on all of us. I can—"

Alannah put her hand on Eddie's arm. "Eddie," she said. "Let's see if this works, okay? If not, I'll be the first to call security."

That resigned Eddie somewhat.

Richard counted silently to 100, then went back inside the medbay. He saw the soldier tense up. He had been imagining as vividly as Eddie, then.

"Do I have to ask you again? I have a job to do elsewhere, so I would prefer it if you stopped wasting my time," Richard said briskly.

"What happens if I answer your questions?" O'Connor asked. He was warming up to the idea. Good.

"That depends on your answers. But," Richard added, "Give me what I want, and getting shipped back to the Terran Defense Force might not be in your cards."

O'Connor closed his eerily blue eyes. Opened them again. "The man who gave me the job goes by the name Egis."

"Human?"

"Yes."

"I don't think I know him," Richard said, tapping his foot impatiently. Making it clear that he needed more than that to even start considering not calling security anyway.

"He contracts me, but he is not the one who wants you dead. He is only a mediator. That is how he works. He never tells me who ordered the job."

"Hm." Richard crossed his arms over his chest and stared up at the ceiling. Of course it was never going to be that easy. "Is this Egis your only employer at the moment, O'Connor?" he asked, looking back down.

"Yes."

"And during your time working for him, how many people have you been contracted to kill?"

For a moment, the soldier didn't reply. Richard dearly hoped the number was not that high.

"Six," came the reply finally.

Richard allowed himself the tiniest of smirks. "Were you as successful with the others as you were with me?"

"No," O'Connor said. "I have never failed before." And then something softer crossed his face. Confusion. Because he had failed now, or because it ought not to be a matter of pride to kill people for money?

"I have to ask," Richard said, "how much is my life worth?"

"50,000 units," O'Connor replied, promptly enough, which meant he really was doing it for the money.

"Honestly, that offends me," Richard replied. He heard Eddie mutter something behind him and Alannah shush her.

"Egis takes a fee," O'Connor said, which was exactly what Richard had hoped for. Not that he cared particularly about the money, but he wanted an opening in the soldier's defense, and here it was.

"Do you enjoy killing?" Richard asked.

Hesitation. Then, "Not particularly."

"I'm going to make you an offer," Richard said. "I don't want to repeat myself, and I am not open for negotiations. Understand?"

"Yes," O'Connor replied. And Richard was pretty sure then that it would play out how he wanted it to.

"Okay. Here's the deal," Richard began. "Your fate is in my hands right now. How would you like to work for me in exchange for my silence? You will help me track down Egis, find out who hired him to make me disappear, and put an end to that by turning them in to the authorities, or whatever it takes. It goes without saying that you will not attempt to kill me again, not during your employ, and not after. And I will not alert anyone to your existence unless you make trouble for me. I will even pay you 10,000 units for your services before we part ways."

A strangled exclamation from Eddie. Richard did not turn.

O'Connor blinked. He did the math, and Richard saw him reach the obvious conclusion that the equation came out in his favor. It was the only way for him to regain his freedom, after all. Granted, the payment Richard was offering was ramyim seeds compared to what Egis paid, but it was enough for him to get very far away from Richard in a comfortable and fast manner after the job was over. "I accept your offer," he said.

Richard clapped his hands together once. "Great. We can probably do this without any paperwork. Oh," he added, "I can't leave you free access to my ship while my colleague and I go back to Dwebl to finish our job there. I'll arrange for more comfortable quarters than these, but I hope you won't mind the inconvenience." He didn't wait for an answer. It didn't much matter either way. Instead, he left the medbay again, feeling anger radiating off Eddie as he passed her.

Once outside in the corridor, she stormed past him to block his way. "What the hell? What the fucking hell are you thinking? You can't hire an assassin who just tried to kill you!"

"I think I just did, though," Richard said.

"I'm not even going to complain about the money, but the kid tried to kill you, and he is running around with illegal implants!"

"Are you sure you can trust him?" Alannah asked, far more calmly than Eddie, but Richard could tell she was agitated as well, only hiding it better.

"I am sure that I can depend on him as far as our agreement goes. After that, we will part. It was never personal, and I'm offering him a deal. He knows there is nothing to be gained from doublecrossing me."

"Unless he uses your trust against you to kill us all and run off with any units available," Eddie said.

"I never said I trusted him," Richard said. "But he wouldn't do that."

"You don't know that! You don't know him!" Eddie argued.

Richard cocked his head. "No. But I'm a pretty good judge of character. Some people might argue that hiring a pilot with a criminal record and a hyper addic—"

"I'm done listening to your urnollshit!" Eddie interrupted him, pointing at him with the dart gun, though it was not a threat as much as an object she happened to have in her hand. "You get yourself killed for all I care. And you can deal with the job on Dwebl on your own. I'm not leaving the *Colibri* with that freak on board." She turned on her heel, effectively stopping further conversation.

Richard turned to Alannah.

"I can't say I agree with your assessment, but it's your call," she said. "Though... Eddie might make you choose between her and him."

Richard sighed. "Are you going to make me choose too?"

She shook her head. "You better make up with Eddie," she said which, Richard knew, was as much of an answer as he was going to get out of her.

If you are throwing a party, you will probably want to provide your guests with snacks. But what to pick if your friends are of multiple species? Your åayu guest is not likely to enjoy a meaty draever morsel, and your average wendek would pick sticking their head in a bottle of zetoi perfume over the poignant smell of traditional human cheese (that is cheese made *by* humans from cow milk, by the way. Not cheese made *from* humans).

Here are five suggestions for snacks that are bound to make your party a success for people of every Category 3 member species!

5: Ramyim.

A safe bet at any party. But you will want somewhere for your guests to discard the outer layer of these delicious seeds. - After interpreting the patterns in them, of course. Even zetois do this for entertainment these days, and they will not see it as cultural appropriation unless you start reading religious meaning into them and/or praying over them.

4: Crack-Shots.

This wendek snack is a small, round and crunchy plant-based mouthful. You can buy ready-made versions all over the galaxy (but beware of discount versions; As a rule, if the expiration date is more than a month away, fresh vegetables have not been involved in the fabrication). Or you can make your own quite easily with a frying pan, a bit of patience, and the right wendek spices.

3: Cucumber sandwiches.

A classic human snack and another safe bet because of their interstellar appeal. The taste isn't striking, but it is wonderfully inoffensive to all Category 3 species' palates. You can purchase preserved cucumber and rehydrate the slices if you don't have access to the fresh kind.

2: Urnoll cheese.

Unlike other kinds of cheese, the urnoll variant is sweet and soft without being sticky and without any offensive aroma. Fermention of urnoll milk is a lengthy process, so you probably want to buy the cheese ready-made. Best served with a dip of your liking and on sticks to easily pop them into your mouth.

1: Sweet kelp peas.

If you haven't tasted this åayu treat, have you even lived? They simply melt in your mouth and leave a fresh and slightly citrus-like sugary aftertaste.

— Alannah Jackson, *Dining with Draevere*

4
YOU'D FUCK UP ALONE

Eddie could have kicked herself in the shin if not for the inefficiency of it, and she wasn't about to ask someone else to do it for her.

Richard Hart was an idiot. A gullible asshole who didn't even realize he was an asshole because he was so distracted by his foot firmly lodged in his mouth. But he was also Eddie's boss. And her friend, a small voice in the back of her head told her. She wanted especially to kick that voice in the shin.

She gave Alannah instructions to carry a shocker with her at all times, keep Eddie as her emergency contact on her patch and not to enter the enhanced murderer's cabin under any circumstances. Then she left the crew quarters and made her way to the nest.

She tossed her backpack onto the seat next to her own in the chick. Eddie preferred its company beside her over Richard's. She put her feet on the console in front of her and pulled up a game from her patch to the main display.

"Hi," Richard said a few minutes later.

Eddie didn't reply. She was so close to breaking her own sober record, and he wouldn't understand a word of what she said if he couldn't see her face.

Richard removed her backpack in the way one would a baby syraxh and sat down next to her, looking at the display.

Eddie ignored him, moved the figures on the display, merging some, scoring more points, momentarily pausing the countdown by getting a particularly neat combo, added golden bars to the stack, and then the timer reached zero.

"Wow," Richard said. "That's impressive."

"We can't all be as crap as you," she muttered. Well, Eddie had a permanent place on the human high score list. She suspected that most, if not all, the top 100 names belonged to pilots and that their records were set while hopped up on hyper like hers. Richard wasn't necessarily crap at it. He was just not trained in the way she was. Even sober, pilots excelled at instinctive thinking in the way puzzle games encouraged.

"I didn't think you were coming," Richard probed.

Eddie finally turned to look at him. "Someone has to fly your ass down there. You also suck at flying." Only half true. He could fly, but he was so slow and careful. Flying with Richard was geriatric.

"Thank you," Richard replied.

"Ready?"

"Yes, all buckled up."

Eddie nodded and removed her feet from the console, swept her hand over the steering module to unlock it and opened the outer doors of the nest.

"Look, I'm sorry for—"

"I'm not here to listen to your excuses," Eddie told him. "I'm here to fly."

Richard took the hint and didn't say anything for the duration of the flight.

"Look," he resumed the conversation after Eddie put the chick down safely on the Dwebl port's landing strip and they were walking toward the clearance area. "I can understand why you are upset."

"Well, that's a relief, at least," she sighed, hating that she had to look at his stupid face to talk to him.

"I appreciate you coming with me. I know you are worried about the ship and Alannah."

Eddie stopped and turned on him. "Your soldier boy is locked up. The *Colibri* and Alannah will be safe. And you are probably right that he will stick to the terms. That's not the problem."

"It's not?" Richard asked, honest surprise painted so clearly on his face that Eddie wanted to slap him.

"No, you dickwad!" Eddie almost shouted. "The problem is that he tried to kill you."

"But he—"

"Shut up and listen!" Eddie snapped. "The problem is that he is a hitman. The problem is you didn't even blink before hiring a cold hearted fucking killer! I have some fucking moral qualms about that."

"Oh," Richard said. At least he had the decency to look taken aback. "Oh, I didn't—"

"Consider that you hired a psycho killer who ought to be locked up? He kills people for money, Richard! I'm not upset that you brought up my history. I know I sucked. But I want to punch you in your goddamn face for suggesting it's the same as him. Are you so high up on your moral horse that you can't see the difference?"

"Are you done?" Richard asked, quietly.

"I don't know!" Eddie shouted. "I don't fucking know if I'm done. I mean, I'm one hundred percent done with your urnollshit, but apart from that..."

Richard held up both of his hands. "Can I just—"

"Justify why you thought it was a good idea not to hand in a criminal to the authorities? Rationalize why the guy who tried to murder you is a great investment? Explain how shooting up on hyper a bit too often is the same as assassinating someone multiple times?

———

33

And I swear, Richard, if you point out that you can only assassinate someone once, I am going to go straight back to the *Colibri* and leave you and your stupid face stranded here!"

"Okay," he said. "I'm sorry. Really. But tell me, how much do you know about the enhanced soldier program?"

"Enough to stay away from them," Eddie muttered, not sure if he caught it and not caring. She began to walk again.

"The military grade artificial body parts are often associated with enhanced soldiers, but prosthetics are not exclusive to the enhanced program, of course," Richard continued, falling into step with her. "If I had lost an arm while I was in the Force, I would have been offered a replacement that might look a lot like his. It would not have violated any treaties."

Eddie made an impatient gesture.

"The enhanced program was something else entirely. The strength of his prosthetic parts exceeds human values, but that's not all. Recruits were altered in other ways. Chances are Kierran O'Connor doesn't... work like normal people do."

"Well, normal people don't kill other people for units," Eddie said and hoped that didn't incite a lecture on how the military worked. It didn't.

"Exactly," Richard said. "The enhanced soldiers were changed. I don't know anything about neurosurgery and biotech, but they were turned into superhumans, physically at least. I'm pretty sure our guest doesn't feel pain in the way we do, and his reactions are faster than they ought to be. And rumors have it that the enhanced also were changed mentally. So—"

"So you are trying to tell me," Eddie interrupted, "that the illegal ex-soldier who tried to kill you wasn't really to blame? That's he's a product of his circumstances? Because that's a nice sob story, but you can't let murderers loose just because they had a bad childhood. They are still accountable for their actions."

"But criminals with a mental illness aren't put in ordinary prisons. They—"

Eddie raised her hands, palms up. "Then find a nice mental hospital for him." She picked up speed and began to consult the map on her patch to end further conversation. She'd said her piece. She didn't need to listen to more of his excuses.

They went back to the area where they had been so thoroughly sidetracked earlier and split up again. Part of Eddie felt reluctant about that, but honestly, how many assassins could be looking for Richard on Dwebl?

All right, on that note... Eddie had to admit to herself at least that she was kind of curious about it all. Despite the fact that Richard was a moron for bringing the enhanced on board the *Colibri*, she supposed she could kind of see where he was coming from. Turning the guy over to the authorities would be the smarter move, but it would probably be a lengthy legal process before it was ever revealed who wanted Richard dead. Eddie could think of a vast number of reasons that Richard could have pissed off someone, but few of them were dire enough to have him killed for.

She shook her head and turned her attention to the surroundings. Right. The street on this low level of the city was empty, but she had been headed to a shop of some kind on her first visit here, and that was still a valid idea. So she sauntered up to the door. A sign in Standard told her she would find anything she needed here. Under it was one in Naiwon's local language that Eddie couldn't read. Presumably it said the same, though.

The door opened, and she stepped inside. Her stomach growled, unprofessionally.

A zetoi was standing at the counter. They looked up from their patch when Eddie entered, but didn't greet her.

Eddie nodded at them and turned to study the selection. Which wasn't great. But there were some snacks from several parts of the galaxy. Even a human chocolate bar. Eddie's stomach growled again.

Why the hell had she not grabbed lunch on the *Colibri*? She would have been able to fume and eat at the same time.

She decided not to go with the chocolate bar after seeing the expiration date which was far overdue. But she wasn't a great fan of zetoi edibles, so she went with a wendek container of bitesized snacks called Crack-Shots.

The small box had the logo from the popular Wendek crime show *Worra & Darith* on it. Not that Eddie watched it much, but she did know that one of the protagonists, the suave and slightly derpy Darith, tended to munch on Crack-Shots, which had increased their popularity through the galaxy. Whether the snack company was making units off the show or vice versa, Eddie had no clue. But someone probably was capitalizing here. Well, the label promised a great flavor and an even greater aroma, the latter not really relevant to human senses. The date on it was two years in the future.

"Hi," Eddie said to the cashier and brandished the snack for them to scan.

"Hey," the bored-looking zetoi said. Their feathers looked dyed, but it was a sloppy job from what Eddie could tell. "30 units."

Eddie held up her patch and transferred the total. It was Richard's fault that she hadn't managed to get lunch. She would get him to pay for this. It made perfect sense. It was part of her search for the escapee. "Have you worked here long?" she asked while pretending to fumble with the packaging of the snack.

"Kinda," the cashier said clacking their bill, the zetoi equivalent to a human shrug.

"I saw you have human snacks," Eddie added, getting the lid off and popping a Crack-Shot into her mouth. "Do you have a lot of human customers?"

"Not really. A few, maybe," the cashier said in the universal tone of a bored teenager, although a zetoi's adolescence came more than a decade later than for humans. "But not tourists like you."

Eddie chose not to explain she wasn't a tourist. "Yeah? I'm looking for a friend who moved here a while back," she said. "But I don't have his exact address. I want to surprise him."

"Okay?" the cashier said, unimpressed.

"Oh," Eddie added as if she had only now come up with this bright idea, "maybe you have seen him around? Here, let me show you..." She pulled up a still of the insurance fraud dude on her patch and flipped it so the cashier could see it.

"Yeah, I've seen him," the cashier said.

"Do you know where he lives? Is it around here?"

"Yeah," the cashier said. "I can't remember where exactly."

Eddie studied them. "Anything I can do to jog your memory? You can have some of these."

The cashier looked down at the Crack-Shots with an uninterested expression. "I hate wendek food," they said. "And besides, I work here. I can just take some if I want to. Which I really don't."

Eddie tapped the toe of her boot impatiently. "Okay. 200 credits to your patch?"

"Okay," the cashier said. "I think I remember where your friend lives. I'm Fanril."

"All right. 200 credits... are on your account now," Eddie said with a theatrical show of swiping the display of her patch. She would get Richard to pay her back for that, too.

The cashier gave her a detailed description of the route to the backyard where the target lived. Eddie thanked them and left the shop, crunching another snack ball between her teeth.

"Got a location on our target. Meet me where I am asap," she said to her patch, trusting it to turn her words into a text message, and added her location to it.

"Be with you in two," came the reply. People never specified which two, but in Eddie's experience, it was never seconds and rarely minutes but some longer unit of unnamed time. So she popped another Crack-Shot into her mouth and sucked on it, periodically taking it out of her mouth to check the color. Like everything else about the wendek, it was aesthetically pleasing.

Richard strode up to her in more like five than two, at least if they were talking minutes. "What have you got?" he asked.

Eddie held out the container to him. "Wendek Crack-Shots. Do you want some?"

"I meant—" he began.

"I know," she interrupted him. "No balls for you, then. I talked to a cashier in a shop who said they had a human customer matching the description. So, our target is supposed to live across the street and down two doors."

"Oh, good. I was afraid you might be standing right outside his window," Richard said with the kind of approval that made Eddie want to whack the back of his head.

"I'm not a moron," she huffed. "So, how do you want to play it?"

"Let's do the polite thing and knock on the front door. See if it's really our guy," Richard said.

"The cashier was pretty sure."

Richard smiled wryly, "I don't doubt it, but all humans look the same, remember?"

"Right," Eddie said.

They walked across the empty street and up to the door. Richard straightened the collar of his jacket. Eddie chased a Crack-Shot around her mouth with her tongue. Richard knocked. They waited.

"So," Eddie said after two actual minutes, "do we break in and make ourselves comfortable while waiting for him to come home, or what?"

Richard studied the door. "There doesn't appear to be any security system in use."

"It's the lowest level of Naiwon. Of course there isn't." Eddie shrugged. "Got a better idea?"

"No. If nothing else, we might be able to learn something about his habits and verify that it's really him."

Eddie shoved the box of snack balls at him. "Here, hold this and cover me."

As Richard moved to shield her from view, Eddie slipped the tools out of her pocket and bent down to work on the lock. She was glad this wasn't a fancy neighborhood with a retina lock or something like that. This was an easy job. Slide in the tool, wiggle it a bit, emit a low energy pulse and turn. Click. She stood up again.

"Well done," Richard said and handed her back the Crack-Shots. "Stand back."

Eddie complied. Since they only had the one dart gun between them and Richard was carrying it this time, she didn't have a weapon. And you never knew how the person inside might react to intruders.

Richard pushed open the door with his shoulder and went in holding the dart gun firmly with both hands as it swung on its hinges.

"Clear," he said after a moment.

Eddie glanced back over her shoulder to make sure no one had seen two humans breaking and entering. Trouble was, someone clearly had. But—

"Richard!" Eddie shouted. No point in explaining anything.

In the street, a lone figure had stopped short, staring at them. And then he whirled around and began to run.

Eddie couldn't be entirely certain he was their quarry. But he was human, he had been headed for this building, and his reaction to seeing them was fleeing. Pretty good odds.

Clutching the Crack-Shots, Eddie set off after him. She didn't shout. It never helped. She had done it the first couple of times she and Richard had to chase someone, and had she really been a fictional detective like Darith, it might have worked, but all it ever did was making her more winded.

The man disappeared between two buildings, and Eddie followed him. She could hear Richard's footsteps pounding the ground behind her, but she had a headstart. She rounded the corner and saw the target up ahead. Damn, she needed to catch up before he emerged into the bigger street. Before he got a chance to disappear into a shop or mingle with a crowd somewhere. But she wasn't catching up fast enough.

Eddie stopped. Plunged her hand into the box of snacks and pulled up a handful. A waste, really, but— She hurled the balls after the man. One of them struck him in the back, uselessly, but the rest tumbled to the ground around him and— Yes! The fugitive yelped, his feet trying to find purchase, his arms flailing hopelessly as he went down.

With a victory whoop, Eddie continued and managed to take hold of the man's hair as he was trying to get back on his feet. She yanked hard, and he shouted at her, his arms windmilling in an attempt to clout her.

Richard had caught up by now and deftly picked the cable strips from her pocket to secure them around the fugitive's wrists. "Lars Olafson," he began, only slightly winded, "we are here on behalf of BrightLife Insurances on the charge of staging your own death and committing insurance fraud. We will take you into custody and bring you back to Yiheyuan Station where you will be put on trial for said offenses."

"Please!" the man cried out. "I needed the money! You don't understand!"

"And I," Eddie said between panting breaths, "needed my Crack-Shots. Tough luck, buddy."

"Did you seriously just trip him with wendek snack balls?" Richard asked under his breath.

"Yep. And on that note," Eddie continued, "you owe me 230 units."

Do you remember that clip of the baby syraxh with the teddy bear on FuzzBot? This one is even better! You have to watch it!

PS: How is your new job going? You haven't even sent me any stills of the pilot or your soldier boss! Come on!!!

PPS: Are they hot?

— Dispatch from Zoe Jackson to Alannah Jackson

Oh, my heart, Zoe! The way the rabbit nuzzles up to the syraxh! Baby animals just make everything better. I watched it three times in a row instead of eradicating typos from the article I'm working on.

You are hopeless, cousin. But... stills included! I'm not going to comment on their potential hotness. That would be unprofessional. I'll let you be the judge. ;)

— Dispatch from Alannah Jackson to Zoe Jackson

5
FuzzBot EXPERIMENT

The door had always been there. When Alannah joined the *Colibri*'s crew, Richard gave her the choice between two cabins that he called unoccupied. It wasn't the word Alannah would use, but then again, the occupants were not human. They were laundry and weapons and other kinds of detritus that tended to accumulate around people like Richard and Eddie. Alannah had picked a cabin, the detritus had been moved elsewhere, and she was currently in the process of making the space look like home by accumulating her own detritus, mainly consisting of knick-knack she picked up in little shops where ever she went.

The door she was staring at now was sealing the entrance to the cabin she hadn't picked. Certain objects had hastily been removed from it today to make it suitable for... Alannah tried to think of a better word than imprisoning and failed. Fine. For imprisoning the enhanced soldier.

Alannah knocked on the door. She wouldn't be able to hear a reply, and the enhanced obviously could not unlock the door for her, but it was still the polite thing to do. She unlocked the door herself and stepped into the doorway. "Hello, Kierran," she said. "May I come in?"

The enhanced soldier was sitting on the cot that unfolded from the wall, his feet on the floor, his hands clasped on his thighs. His back was straight, and he looked like a caged animal that might leap to his feet and attack at any provocation. "Yes," he replied tonelessly.

Alannah tried for a smile. "My name is Alannah."

"Yes," he said again.

Right. Richard had told him earlier. Alannah cleared her throat. "I thought you might be hungry. So I brought you something to eat and drink."

Kierran O'Connor's eyes flicked to the tray in her hands and back to her face.

"You... Um, you do eat and drink, right?" she said. Surely, he was biological enough to need that.

"Yes," he said for the third time. But a quick expression stole onto his face. Amusement?

"Good. You have to promise me something, though," she continued.

"What?"

Not much of a talker. "You have to promise me not to do anything... rash. Like hitting me with the tray or..." She shrugged awkwardly.

The enhanced soldier blinked. "I promise," he said.

Alannah studied him for another moment. If he had wanted to, he could probably have killed her already. If he was really as dangerous as Richard seemed to think. And Eddie... Eddie who had told Alannah not to go anywhere near the murderous freak, her words, while she and Richard were gone. But... The thing was that Richard had made it completely clear that Alannah was to follow his orders if she joined the crew. And it had been Eddie telling her explicitly not to go near Kierran. Not Richard. Alannah did feel a bit guilty, but when she sat down to eat alone in the galley, it felt wrong.

Just... wrong. So she had laden the tray with food for both of them and come here.

Looking at him now, she felt it was the right thing to do. Even if part of her was scared of him, and another part of her was very much aware that he was a murderer, it was still the right thing. Maybe it was because he looked so young.

Alannah stepped closer and held out the tray for him. "Please hold this a moment."

He took it and sat perfectly still.

Alannah removed a stack of boxes from a small table, pushed it closer to the cot and took the tray again. She placed it on the table. Then she took a sturdy box and dragged it toward the table. She sat down across from Kierran, discreetly moving the shocker in her waistband.

"Please," she said, hoping her smile didn't look too nervous. "Help yourself."

The boy stared at the food. His blue eyes narrowed.

"It's not poisoned," Alannah said and picked up a cracker, dipped it in the urnoll cheese dressing and put it in her mouth.

"Why?" Kierran enquired.

"Why it's not poisoned?" Alannah asked around the mouthful of delicious fermented urnoll milk.

"No," he said. "Why are you doing this?"

"Because," Alannah said slowly, "I thought you must be hungry. We don't just lock people up and starve them around here." Eddie had seemed perfectly happy with doing that, though. And Richard had neglected to ask Alannah to feed the prisoner. Well, at least *she* wasn't in the habit of starving people.

Kierran picked up a cracker, studied it, then brought it to his mouth and bit into it.

"You are welcome to the cheese as well," Alannah said.

He didn't reply. Only chewed the cracker. Okay then.

"Do you want to tell me a bit about yourself?" she ventured.

Kierran stared at her with badly concealed surprise. "No," he said.

"You know," Alannah said, pouring two glasses of water and ignoring the slight trembling of her hands, "it's customary to do a bit of smalltalk when your host shows an interest in you."

He looked like he'd swallowed something sour.

Alannah held the glass of water just out of his reach. "Where did you grow up? Do you have any hobbies? How old are you?"

A short moment of hesitation. "Yellowstone, no, 25," he then said.

Alannah suppressed a sigh and held out the glass to him. Somehow, she didn't feel like she was sitting next to a dangerous criminal. It was more like trying to coax a frightened, aggressive animal to trust her by bribing it with food. 25. Not quite a boy, then, but still too young to— Well, there wasn't really a right age to become an assassin for hire. But 25 was definitely too young to be the kind of person that Kierran was.

"I lived on Yellowstone for a short while," Alannah offered. "Though I did a lot of traveling back then too. When did you—" She cut herself off. She wanted to ask him about the prosthetics. About becoming an enhanced soldier. Why he had done it. How old he was then. Why he hadn't been dismantled when the program was terminated. Why he had decided to pursue such a horrible career path. But if she pushed too hard, he would curl in on himself and refuse to talk at all. A change of strategy, then.

"Richard likes to watch old science fiction movies from Earth. From before hyper technology was invented. He says they have historical value, but I think he secretly likes to gloat over everything they got wrong," she said.

Kierran continued to stare at her.

"Eddie plays games on her patch. She competes against other pilots on the high score lists. You know, they all have amazing reflexes. Regular people wouldn't stand a chance against them."

Alannah smiled and took a sip of her own water. Then concentrated on eating.

"And you?" Kierran asked.

Alannah did her best not to smirk. "Cute animal clips on FuzzBot," she said. Not her only hobby, but the one that fit into her scheme now. "You know the kind. A syraxh licks a rabbit and snuggles with it, oblivious to the fact that it could pounce and eat it."

Kierran's face looked even more blank than his default setting.

"You don't watch cute animal clips?" she asked.

"No."

"But you know the kind I'm talking about, right?"

Kierran frowned as if this was something he had to think hard about. "I don't remember," he finally said.

That, Alannah thought, was an interesting choice of words. Did he have a lot of holes in his memory? She filed the knowledge for later, although she recognized what her brain was trying to do. She was trying to make excuses for him. Trying to find a reason for his being a murderer. Not that a lack of cute animal clips necessarily damaged a person's emotional life, but... She was well aware that this was ridiculous. Showing someone clips of funny animals wouldn't break down their defenses and make them realize the error of their ways. But still. Her intuition told her this boy was not used to being treated like a person, and maybe... just maybe, doing exactly that would make a small dent in his defenses.

"Okay, let me show you," she said. She moved to the other side of the table and sat down next to him.

Kierran's whole body tensed. For a moment, Alannah thought he might strike at her, or at least stand up to get away from her. But he didn't move.

It took a while to load FuzzBot. She really needed to get a new patch soon. But finally, she managed to bring up one of her favorite compilations on the display.

For the next five minutes, they sat in a silence that was only broken by involuntary little "awws" on her part and the occasional

<hr>

chatter by the animals. Cats, dogs, syraxhs, rabbits and keng paraded across the display in succession doing cute animal things.

Alannah shot a glance at Kierran's profile. He looked concentrated. Not exactly about to break into tears over the cuteness, but at least he was staring intently at the display.

"How was that?" she asked after the short clip compilation ended.

Kierran breathed in. "I... don't know," he said. He sounded honest.

"Okay. Maybe you need to watch more in order to form an opinion," Alannah suggested.

He looked at her sharply, but she really did mean it.

"I have to go now, though." She stood up and picked up the tray, erasing the signs of her disobedience.

She had made it all the way to the door when he spoke up.

"Thank you," he said.

Alannah turned and smiled. She wondered if he knew what he was really thanking her for. "You're welcome," she said and left it at that.

An hour later, the chick returned to the *Colibri*. Richard was marching a stranger out of the nest by the time Alannah made it there. She had decided to walk really, really slowly in order to avoid a potential shouting match between him and Eddie upon their return. But judging from Richard's contented look and Eddie sauntering out of the nest right behind him with a box of wendek snacks in her hand, Alannah hadn't needed to worry that much.

"Hello," Alannah greeted everybody. If you subtracted the beard, the stranger looked very much like the still the insurance company had provided. "I take it the job went well?"

The stranger glared at her but didn't say anything.

"Yes, without a hitch," Richard said.

"Everything okay here? He hasn't done anything?" Eddie practically interrupted him, studying Alannah as if expecting a knife to stick out of her abdomen.

"Yes," Alannah confirmed with a smile. "Everything is fine." She wasn't going to elaborate.

"I'll escort our new guest somewhere safe and comfortable," Richard said. "And then we will coordinate the next step with O'Connor."

"You do that, Dick," Eddie muttered. "This ship needs more prison cells."

"Drop the sarcasm, Eddie," Richard said although his back was already turned.

"You can't tell if I was being sarcastic!" she retorted.

Which he obviously couldn't process either.

"Idiot," Eddie said and crunched a Crack-Shot between her teeth. "Want one?"

"Thank you." Alannah put her hand in the offered box and fished one out. Okay, so Eddie and Richard were not entirely back to normal, though their normal also did include a lot of bickering.

"So he really hasn't tried anything?" Eddie said as the two of them began the walk toward the impromptu prison cell.

"Really," Alannah confirmed. "He's locked up, remember?" She almost added that even if he hadn't been, she was pretty sure he would not have done anything, but that was skirting too close to the truth she wanted to keep quiet.

"Hm," Eddie said. Disappointedly? Did she actually want Kierran to have been trying to escape? Yes, Alannah realized, she did. Because that would mean she was right and Richard was wrong. Sometimes the two of them acted like five-year-olds.

They waited outside the door for Richard, and he turned up only a couple of minutes later.

"Our newest guest is in the galley. I cuffed him to a table," Richard said.

"Awesome. Can't wait to have dinner while he glares at me," Eddie said flatly.

"I want him off the ship as quickly as possible," Richard continued. "The question is whether we can do that and get to wherever O'Connor's employer is located rapidly enough to stick to one dose of hyper."

"Probably, if you don't have to spend hours bragging about how I caught him to our contractor," Eddie said.

Richard shook his head, but he didn't rise to the bait. "Okay. Let's go make a plan." He unlocked the door and frowned at the panel.

Alannah swallowed. He could not possibly tell it had been unlocked before. Could he?

Well, whatever the case, Richard didn't comment. He strode into the cabin. "Hello, O'Connor," he said briskly. "How are you enjoying your stay on the *Colibri*?"

Kierran leapt to his feet, his posture more alert and poised to fight than when Alannah had last seen him. His gaze went from Richard to Alannah and back again without any indication that they had been looking at cute animal clips together. Which was for the better, of course.

"I have no complaints," he said, looking like he very much had complaints.

"Good," Richard continued, walking further into the cabin flanked by Eddie. Alannah stayed in the background. "We are almost ready to leave this system and pay your Egis a visit."

Kierran nodded.

"So let's have the details." Richard made an encouraging gesture. "Who is he? Where do we find him?"

"Egis is human. Around 60 years old, white, dark brown but greying short hair, 182 centimeters tall and weighs approximately 89 kilograms. One of his ears sits half a centimeter higher than the other, and he dresses in fashionable clothes with a preference for green," Kierran said, which was oddly precise. Was that an enhanced thing? "He operates from the Hawking system, usually from the planet itself, but he recently changed his location to Stonehenge Station."

"Stonehenge?" Alannah exclaimed. "Oh, for the love of—" She swallowed the rest of her objection to the unfairness of the universe. Stonehenge of all places. That was where her now completely destroyed former employer used to have their main office. It was where some secret person had hired Richard and Eddie for the mission that brought her into their company. She really had no desire to go back there anytime soon. It reminded her too much of having her career ruined.

Eddie crossed her arms over her chest and looked at Richard.

Richard's mouth had become a very thin line. "It's a big station," he said to Kierran, though Alannah had a feeling it was directed just as much at his team. "We're going to need a bit more than that."

"Egis will be armed, but he is no challenge on his own," Kierran said. "He will also have at least one bodyguard with him and another somewhere in the vicinity scouting for trouble."

"Noted," Richard said. "And where on Stonehenge does he reside?"

Kierran was quiet for a moment. "What happens after you have his location?" he asked.

"Then we go there and deal with him. Extract information regarding the person who hired him to hire you. And we hand him over to the authorities," Richard said. "After that, the arrangement between you and me is done, I transfer your 10,000 units, and you are free to go, as I already specified."

A flicker of an expression crossed Kierran's face. "I am not going to give you his address," he said.

"Oh, yes you are, you little twat!" Eddie burst out.

Richard made a shooing motion at her, which made her seethe even more. "Why?" he asked Kierran.

"I have no guarantee that you won't prematurely terminate our agreement... and me."

"You have my word," Richard said.

50

Kierran shook his head. "I will go with you to Stonehenge and show you Egis' location," he said.

"How does that change anything? If we wanted to, we could just kill you there instead," Eddie huffed.

"Eddie," Richard said, warningly.

Eddie looked at Alannah for support.

"Not helpful," Alannah murmured and patted her arm.

"All right," Richard said. "I get it. You go with us to Stonehenge. I'll return for you when we are there."

Kierran gave one short nod of acknowledgment. "You will also need my retina scan to get into the building he lives in," he added.

"We could just pop out your eye for that," Eddie muttered under her breath. Alannah didn't think Richard saw it, and if Kierran heard it, he didn't react. She also doubted Eddie would go that far.

"You just rolled over and let him have his way!" Eddie accused Richard once they were back in the hallway.

"Only because it makes sense from his perspective and we won't lose anything by complying."

"Unless he decides to turn on us the moment he sees that Egis guy and they join forces," Eddie argued.

"He won't. How do you think Egis will react to the whole thing? Probably not by trusting O'Connor."

"But why does he want to go in the first place? Eddie is right, you could just kill him on Stonehenge if you wanted to," Alannah said.

"Better odds," Richard said. "There are no witnesses as long as we are on board the *Colibri*, and nowhere for him to flee to."

"Oh." Alannah considered that. "I'm strangely glad I don't think like you," she added.

"You should be," Richard said. "It's a luxury not to have to."

"Well, that went from åayu documentary to draever extreme sports clip at hyper speed," Eddie noted.

If you have followed recent local news even sporadically, you will be aware that General Webb, the Terran Defense Force head of military security on Stonehenge Station, recently passed away very suddenly. So sad. Lots of hugs and comfort ice cream to his family.

But fear not! Living up to their motto of "we do things fast so we might regret them later", the TDF has already appointed a new head of military security to Stonehenge. Just kidding. I'm sure our station's new de facto leader will be great.

Here's the run-down of what we know: Surprisingly, the TDF did not bring in another general for us. We are getting a colonel, and a pretty young one, too. It turns out to be one Colonel Micah Dietrich who, like General Webb, is an intelligence officer. To the uninitiated, that doesn't only mean they are smart, although they probably have to be that too. They're actually just glorified data analysts. Or spies!

I did some digging, and it's really hard to find any dirt— I mean, info on Dietrich. According to my sources, they rose through the ranks really fast because of some super classified field missions, whatever that means. Did they spy on separationists? Assassinate an ambassador of a foreign species? Or... what? Whatever the truth may be, you have to wonder why someone who is that amazing at being a field agent is suddenly getting a deskjob here.

But I'll let you make up your own mind because I had the brief pleasure of running into our station's new boss earlier today when I happened to be walking by the TDF headquarters. Have a look at this clip.

Emery: "Colonel Dietrich! Over here!"
Dietrich: "Yes?"
Emery: "I'm Emery. You may have heard of me."
Dietrich: "... I don't believe I have."

Emery: "I was on *Stonehenge Kiss and Tell*. I run *Red Trend Alert* and *FuzzBot Fail*. I'm pretty big on VoidNet. No?"

Dietrich: "I see. Can I help you with anything?"

Emery: "Do you have any comments on the rumors surrounding General Webb's tragic death?"

Dietrich: "You will have to enlighten me to the nature of said rumors."

Emery: "Oh, you know how it is. Just suspicious of him to die so suddenly. Do you think there was any foul play involved? Foreign powers wanting him out of the way?"

Dietrich: "General Webb passed away from natural causes after a short period of illness. Rest assured that there is no uncertainty in the matter."

Emery: "All right, then. On a *completely* different note, you are going to be the new head of military security on Stonehenge Station. That's a pretty big deal! How does that make you feel?"

Dietrich: "I am confident that my staff and I will continue to ensure the stability that General Webb has given this station."

Emery: "Of course. I heard you are married. How is this sudden promotion going to affect your marriage?"

Dietrich: "I don't believe my personal life to be of any consequence to my work here. Now, if you will excuse me —"

Emery: "Is there anything you want to say to my viewers? I'll just remind you this is a big chance for you to reach a huge audience. Really connect with the public."

Dietrich: "There will be an official public announcement tomorrow at 1200 hours. Now, please allow me to pass."

Emery: "Sure. No need to get cranky about it."

Well then, that's Colonel Dietrich. Crisp uniform, beautiful hair, gorgeous green eyes. I give our new military leader 10/10 for style, 10/10 for looks, I mean, they could be a model, am I right? And a mere 4/10 for personality. But I'm sure we are all in for an interesting time with them on the military throne.

Next up: What's up with the new high-waisted pants trend? Don't hide those gorgeous hip bones. But first, a word from my sponsors, Starlite Planetary Guides.

— Clip from the archive of self-proclaimed local news reporter/voidfluencer and PlaNet celebrity Emery

6
AGAINST THE ODDS

Stonehenge Station was not the center of the known universe. Granted, as the space station orbiting one of the first and largest human planetary settlements, it was an important hub of communication, transport and commerce. But it was still only one of many locations in a vast galaxy.

Richard would have felt better if Egis resided just about anywhere else. If he did, Kierran O'Connor need never set foot on Stonehenge where someone might recognize Richard and ask questions he did not want to answer. But, Richard told himself, the odds of running into Colonel Dietrich were staggeringly low. And apart from their adjutant, no one else knew about Richard's relation to them. The Lieutenant was even blissfully in the dark regarding the details of their previous cooperation.

Alannah decided to stay on the *Colibri* instead of going sightseeing while the rest of them took care of business. In her words, she had had enough of Stonehenge for a lifetime. Richard didn't blame her.

"All right. Let's go," Richard said to his team when the pipeline that, according to O'Connor, would bring them close to Egis' location arrived at the platform. He led the way into the pipeline car. It was half full. Mostly human passengers, staring off into space or occupied with their patches or looking at the advertisement clips looping on the displays overhead. One wendek in a facemask, a couple of åayu talking quietly. No one paid very much attention to Richard and his little group.

O'Connor stepped into the pipeline after Richard. His survey of the car resembled Richard's own. He was wearing black clothing including gloves covering his artificial hand, and his face had almost healed from the fight on Dwebl with the help of the nanobots in his body, no doubt. His eyes were alert and probably took in more than normal human sight would. Eddie brought up the rear. She looked pissed. Which she was. She had argued that there must be a way to ditch O'Connor and take care of this on their own. But Richard had no leverage of any value to convince the enhanced soldier to give up Egis' location.

"Has any of you ever gone to the beach on Hawking?" Richard asked. Eddie and O'Connor were being awfully conspicuous just glaring at each other. Better to strike up conversation. Make it sound like they were tourists.

"Yeah," Eddie said.

Richard, knowing he wouldn't get much more out of her, turned to O'Connor. "What about you?"

"No."

"The sand is pink," Richard continued, conversationally. "Not rosy grey, but actually pink. It's due to the planet's geology."

None of them looked impressed. Richard found himself wishing Alannah had come along for this trip, after all.

"Since when are you interested in rocks aside from whiskey on them?" Eddie asked.

"I read about it in the guide," Richard replied. "There were lots of fun facts about Hawking. For instance, parts of the original settlement is modeled on iconic buildings from London on Earth."

Eddie and O'Connor continued to look unimpressed. As far as undercover agenting went, they both had a long way to go.

Luckily, their stop came up quickly, and the three of them left the pipeline. Richard gave up chatting and took the lead once more.

"O'Connor?" he asked when they stepped off the platform.

"That way." O'Connor indicated the direction with a nod of his head.

Richard consulted the map on his patch. They were heading away from the more overtly commercial parts of the station with storefronts and restaurants and tourist-friendly signs. Apparently, they were going to Amesbury, one of the areas that housed the permanent residents of Stonehenge. The civilian residents, at least. Usually the Force would locate its staff closer to the military headquarters.

Stonehenge was a largely egalitarian station. There were no slums to speak of and no neighborhoods that reeked of excessive wealth. Sure, some restaurants were more expensive than others, and there were economical differences between groups of inhabitants, but compared to so many other places, this station had managed to stick to the dream of the people who built it fairly well.

O'Connor guided them down one broad street and veered off through a narrower and less populated pathway. "Up there," he said.

Richard considered the building in front of them. It took up all the vertical space in this part of the station, which was rather a lot, and although it was typical, utilitarian space station architecture, there were gilded embellishments to it suggesting that whoever lived here had a lot of units and pretty bad taste.

Eddie whistled and said something that might be a sarcastic quip about the building, or genuine awe.

"Which floor?" Richard asked O'Connor.

The enhanced soldier hesitated before he answered, "Third floor."

Despite keeping an eye out for Egis' people, Richard had not been able to spot anyone who looked like they may be carrying concealed weapons, and he was not sure if this was a good or a bad sign. "All clear to go in?" he asked O'Connor to have his assessment confirmed.

"Yes," O'Connor said with a slightly puzzled look.

Getting into the building was simple enough. O'Connor merely stepped up to the scanner at the door and waited for it to register him. Then the door opened, and they all went in.

They rode the elevator up to the third floor in silence. Richard discreetly checked his weapons, and he saw Eddie do the same. O'Connor was unarmed, though from personal experience, Richard knew that by no means rendered him harmless.

"Left or right?" Richard asked O'Connor. "It's time for specifics."

"Left. It's the suite at the far end of the corridor. A bodyguard will be posted outside the door."

"I take point," Richard said. "Kierran after me, Eddie brings up the rear again." He trusted her to neutralize Kierran if he made any move to attack either of them. "I take the guard out, and then you take care of the lock, Eddie."

"Aye, aye, Captain," she said.

The elevator dinged. Now came the action. Richard took a deep breath.

The elevator door opened, Richard stepped out— and immediately froze. Damn. He spun on his heel. "Back down!" he hissed.

"What?" Eddie asked from behind Kierran.

"Go!" he continued. "Just go and keep an eye on Kierran."

Kierran was looking utterly confused. There was no way he could have known this. And also no way this in any shape or form would be to his personal advantage.

Eddie opened her mouth to argue, but quickly realized it was an order. She nodded and backed into the elevator, quickly followed by the enhanced soldier.

Richard turned around again, composing his face into something resembling that of a man with nothing to hide.

At the far end of the corridor, exactly where Egis ought to be located, two uniformed soldiers stood with their backs to him. They appeared to be in the process of handcuffing three others who were sitting on the floor. One of those, Richard realized, was a man matching O'Connor's particular description of Egis.

Richard made his way toward the group, but before he managed to address any of the soldiers, a third uniformed person appeared in the doorway, peeling off a pair of forensic gloves. They were shorter than the average soldier, slender, perfectly poised, and with a mane of whitish hair in a thick braid. The officer said something to the others. Then stopped in their tracks and turned to Richard.

And although Richard had the advantage of a few seconds on them, they greeted him completely and utterly nonplussed. "Ah, good day, Captain Hart."

"Colonel Dietrich," Richard returned with a nod, trying to match the nonchalance of the head of Stonehenge military security.

One of Dietrich' people turned to them with an inquiring expression.

"Thank you, Captain Najjar," Dietrich told her. "Please take it from here. I will join you shortly."

"Yes, Colonel," the Captain said. "Let's go," she continued to the trio on the floor, yanking up one of the men by the handcuffs. He appeared to have been darted in both knees and could hardly stand.

Colonel Dietrich waited for their people to clear out. Then they turned to Richard again. "I assume you are here on a professional errand?" they asked. Straight to the heart of the matter.

Richard nodded. "Yes. I... needed to talk to the man your people just apprehended."

"What a coincidence," Dietrich said. "I should very much like to know more about that."

And Richard would very much like to know more about Dietrich's own interest. A military raid on Egis' quarters involving Dietrich themself meant it had to be a big deal. It also explained why there had been no guards outside, come to think of it.

"I was tipped off that he sent an assassin after me," Richard ventured.

Dietrich's eyes narrowed ever so slightly. "Tipped off?" they repeated.

"In a manner of speaking," Richard insisted. "Or rather, someone hired him to send an assassin after me."

"There is more to that story, I'm sure," the Colonel remarked.

"I assume you are here for a similar reason," Richard stood his ground.

"Well, no one sent an assassin after me, Captain," Dietrich said, a sharp smile tugging at their lips.

No, Richard thought. Rumor had it that Dietrich had been an assassin themself, though one who worked for the Force. Richard managed not to say this out loud. But dammit, how was he going to get to the bottom of this now that the Force was involved? There was no doubt Dietrich would interrogate Egis and go after everyone who had contracted him. They would probably also go after any hired guns of his, which included Kierran. Which, Richard reminded himself, was none of his business. As long as he didn't rat on the enhanced soldier, he was not breaking the terms of their agreement.

"Perhaps we should talk somewhere private," he suggested.

"I agree," Dietrich said. "Would you care to join me in my office?"

"Yes," Richard replied, feeling that the invitation was somehow a power move, although he could not put his finger on exactly how.

It turned out that Dietrich had one of the Force's cars waiting around the corner from the building. Richard didn't recognize the driver.

"I need to send my associate a message. She'll be wondering where I've gone," Richard said, casually, as he slipped onto the backseat.

"Of course." Dietrich leaned back in their seat next to the driver, bringing up their own patch.

There was a message from Eddie waiting on Richard's patch. "What the hell??" it said. Nothing more.

Obviously, Richard would need to write his reply. He couldn't let Dietrich know about Kierran. "The Force got Egis. I'll negotiate for information. Keep our friend away from authorities and stand by until further notice."

Richard looked back up. Dietrich was moving their fingers across the display floating above their patch, and Richard had a moment to compose himself and try to figure out how to play this one. He studied the Colonel. A few strands had come loose from Dietrich's braided hair and spilled over their ever so slightly flushed face. Richard wished he could turn back time a few hours, and not only because he would have liked to see the Colonel in action. He also really wanted to know what had happened to set the Force on Egis, and how much Dietrich knew about his affairs.

The car stopped outside the Force's headquarters, and Dietrich exchanged a few words with the driver before entering.

The adjutant was sitting at his desk outside Dietrich's office. He looked up from his work when they entered. "Welcome back, Colonel. Did the—" His gaze flicked to Richard and back again. "Did the operation go as planned?"

The Colonel said something else as they passed the desk.

"No, only a report from Lieutenant Ndiaye," the adjutant replied.

Richard nodded at the Lieutenant in greeting and followed Dietrich into their office.

"So," the Colonel said as they sat down and waved at the empty chair for Richard. "You were going to tell me your side of this case."

He would rather not. But with Egis in the Colonel's custody, he would obviously have to say something. Richard cleared his throat. "I was pursuing a case on Dwebl," he said, "and an assassin surprised me. It was unrelated to my case there."

Dietrich gestured for him to go on.

"It became clear that it was the person you apprehended who hired the assassin, though he was only a middleman."

"Yes," the Colonel agreed. "We have had our eyes on him for a while. He facilitates assassinations for clients who want someone out of the way. And what were you going to do when you found him?"

"The same thing I imagine you are going to do," Richard ventured.

Dietrich smiled. "Oh, do you have access to aletheia?" they asked, silkily.

"No," Richard said. The drug was more restricted than hyper and just as hard to reverse engineer and copy. For him to have it would mean he had a connection in the Force who illegally supplied him. "I intended to make use of a more direct approach." He had intended to put a gun to Egis' head and make threats, that was what.

"Hm." Dietrich steepled their fingers in front of them. "I feel compelled to inquire where the assassin is at this point."

"He escaped," Richard said promptly. "I managed to extract limited information from him, but..." He clenched his jaw, then unclenched it. Lying through his teeth to what would have been his superior officer in another life felt wrong. But he had made a deal with O'Connor. Handing him over to Dietrich would be a smart move, but Richard did not want to break his word. And besides, he might very well need the enhanced soldier's help with the person who wanted him dead as per their agreement.

"How unfortunate," Dietrich said. If they had any misgivings about the explanation, they chose not to share them. "And so, in this hypothetical scenario, what would you do next?"

"It was my intention to track down the person who wants me dead and settle matters," Richard said. He really didn't appreciate feeling like he was the one being interrogated.

"Settle matters," Dietrich echoed. "Indeed a direct approach."

"I would bring them to the authorities, of course. I'm a reputable investigator, not a vigilante with an itching trigger finger," Richard supplied, trying not to sound as irritated as he felt.

Another quickly concealed smile. "Of course," Dietrich said. "Well, my analysts will go through the data on Egis' patch if it isn't—" They cut themself off again, touched their patch, and held up a finger to keep Richard from talking. Or bolting.

"Yes, Lieutenant?" they said.

A disembodied voice that may or may not belong to their adjutant began to explain something. Richard had a feeling that if he had been able to decipher the words, Dietrich would not have taken the message with him in the room.

"I see. Thank you, Lieutenant," the Colonel said. Their lips compressed into a thin, dismayed line. "Well," they continued to Richard, "it appears that Egis' patch was indeed set to delete everything on it the moment it was taken off his wrist."

Which meant there was no readily available information about his clients or his hired guns. Damn.

"We can trace some activities, of course, but it will take time. It's been a while since I conducted an aletheia interrogation on a civilian," Dietrich added.

Richard drummed his fingers on his thigh. "I have some time to kill, if you need an assistant," he said.

"I'm sure I can cope on my own," Dietrich said. "However, I think that, given the situation, you had better stay here until I have finished. Have you had lunch?"

"No," Richard admitted.

"I'll have my adjutant escort you to the mess hall," the Colonel decided. "I'll notify you as soon as the case progresses."

"Thank you," Richard said. He had no doubt the Colonel was keeping him around for their own gain, but at least he would get some more information out of it. And free lunch.

To most of us, whether we live in the human diaspora or not, spaceships and stations and planetary settlements feel natural. Like something that has been around forever. But if we look at the larger perspective, space travel is relatively new. Humanity did not even set foot on Earth's very own Moon until the middle of the 20th century, and even after that, it would be centuries before space travel wasn't restricted to only the extremely few, the astronauts who went through rigorous training to be able to stand the spaceflight conditions of those eras.

It makes sense, though. We did not have a way to efficiently create artificial gravity, we did not have the pelso plating that flawlessly shields our ships from the background radiation of space. We also did not have the right tools to planetform foreign worlds to make them habitable for us. But perhaps most importantly, we did not have faster-than-light travel. The distance from our native solar system to even the closest star was hard to grasp. And to another solar system with planets that might be or be able to become habitable? Even more unfathomable.

Of course, it was only after countless experiments, some of which went fatally wrong, that humanity found a way to safely travel through hyperspace, partly due to the drug pilots take to enhance their processing speed and senses when jumping. Even then, the first ships didn't as much sail through hyperspace as bounce, from what historical clips and texts tell us.

As we all know, it was not long after we began to efficiently travel out of our own solar system that other technologically advanced species contacted us. I don't know about you, but it feels humbling to me to know that they were out there all along, settling on distant planets and forging diplomatic alliances before we even reached our own Moon. And not only were they out there; they also knew about us and had Earth marked on every star chart as a restricted planet until we became capable of hyperspace travel. Until they had to confront us. Some may argue that we, as a species, were not nearly as mature and ready to be part of an interstellar community as other species. I am not one to deny that, but I think we grew up quickly. We had to. And I think it was for the better. Humanity has never been as united and internally peaceful as we are now.

— Alannah Jackson, *The Human Legacy*

7

BABYSITTING

Eddie groaned and scowled at her patch as if giving it a dirty look might change the message from Richard. It didn't. "The Force got Egis. I'll negotiate for information. Keep our friend away from authorities and stand by until further notice." That was all it said.

Eddie turned her glare on the enhanced soldier instead. He looked as annoyingly blank and indifferent as ever. "We have to wait," she said by way of explanation. "Are you hungry?"

"No."

She sighed. Richard's message was vague as hell. No estimated time frame, no meeting place, no nothing. And everything about this was needlessly complicated. There was no reason Richard couldn't just hand the assassin over to the authorities and let them sort out the whole mess. Let them track down Egis as well as the person who wanted Richard dead. But of course he couldn't do that. He was Richard Hart. He had to poke at everything with a stick and get involved personally in matters that could be handled by other people perfectly well. Maybe it was a military thing. Maybe it was paranoia. Maybe it was just that he was a control freak.

"Okay, come on," Eddie said to the enhanced... No, Kierran. If they were going to appear even remotely as if they were were casually hanging out, she needed to start thinking of him as Kierran. She looked him over. "And stop looking like a criminal," she added. It wasn't only his clothes. She wore plenty of black too, although his gloves did look a bit off on a perfectly temperate space station. He just had a furtive air about him. "You must be the worst undercover agent ever."

"I'm not an—" he began.

"Well," Eddie all but snapped, "you are now. Until Richard gets back to me, the two of us are going to kill some time and nothing else, and we are undercover as two average people hanging out on Stonehenge waiting for a ship to somewhere. Got it?"

"Yes," Kierran said.

"Step one," Eddie told him, "Stop giving me monosyllablic answers! Talk like a normal person. Or, you know what I mean." Alannah would call that phrasing ableist, Eddie thought. But she wasn't talking about abilities here. She was talking about Kierran being deliberately obtuse.

He didn't so much glare at her as continued to regard her with that even, uninterested stare.

"Step two; Look alive!" she continued, adding some gesticulation to emphasis what she meant. "Come on. Let's go sightseeing. And try to look like you are marginally enjoying it."

They went back to the pipeline and took it a few stops. Eddie consulted her patch. There were plenty of options on a big station like Stonehenge. But one of the advertisements in the pipeline caught her attention, so she decided to go with that. "How do you feel about history?" she asked Kierran.

"I don't," he said and then, maybe remembering her order to stop with the monosyllables, "feel anything either way."

"Is that right?" Eddie said between gritted teeth. She was pretty sure that was a general statement and nothing to do with history. Cold-hearted killing machine, that's what he was. But a cold-hearted killing machine whom it was somehow her job to babysit until Richard got his head out of the Terran Defense Force's ass.

They left the pipeline at the stop closest to the exhibition area. It was a public space, but probably not one where anyone would think to look for an assassin on the run, or whatever Kierran was at this point. Honestly, Eddie was as indifferent to history as Kierran was, but this was free, and it was something to do where she could easily keep an eye on him. And where he couldn't do any harm without attracting a lot of unwanted attention.

She scanned her patch at the info stand. Kierran did not scan his patch. Well, that made sense, she supposed. Still, just looking at the exhibition without getting any context was kind of suspicious. Eddie pulled out her earbuds and handed one to Kierran. "Here," she said.

He looked at it as if she was offering him a Crack-Shot that had already been in and out of her mouth ten times.

"I don't have wendek ear lice or anything. Take it," Eddie ordered.

"Wendek... ear... lice?" Kierran repeated.

"Yeah, or whatever. Look, my ears are so healthy I don't even know what diseases they could theoretically have."

"I am not worried about that. My system cleanses any infections," Kierran said, stringing together the longest monologue so far. It was almost overwhelming. Almost.

"Lucky you!" Eddie said, trying to sound cheerful because three people were walking past them into the exhibition area. But by the look of it, they were so engrossed in the displays that they paid no attention to Eddie and Kierran. "See," Eddie whispered, "that's how we want to look."

The person in the middle slipped her arm around one of her companions, hugging them close to her, and then leaning in to kiss the other.

"Well, not like that," Eddie added.

Kierran looked mildly offended that she would even suggest he might have an ounce of affection stuffed away in him.

They proceeded to look at the exhibition. The first part was about prehistoric Hawking. Or pre-human Hawking, Eddie supposed. After looking at lumps of rocks that were all either boring, pretty or weird, they moved on to the tale of how humanity created a space station in orbit around the planet and then began to settle on it. The guided tour voice in Eddie's ear was very excited about all of it and reminded her of Alannah's attitude to... everything. This might actually have been a fun trip if it had been Alannah with her and not Kierran. Alannah would probably know most of it already. And she would be excited to learn new things and eager to share her own thoughts on them.

Eddie shot a look at Kierran. At least he appeared to be listening and studying the displays. Not in the way that Alannah would, though. More like he expected there to be a quiz later.

The exhibition went from facts about planetforming, something humanity didn't have to do a lot of on Hawking, to the establishment of cities and what was necessary to have in a settlement, like a university, a hospital and an art gallery.

Kierran lingered at the cluster of art created by early settlers to study a painting that was, apparently, made with pigment from local sources instead of imported ones.

"Into art?" Eddie asked.

Kierran's expression closed up as if he had been caught doing something bad or super private. He shook his head and quickly moved on.

Eddie didn't know what that was about, and also didn't care, so she didn't pursue the matter.

They went on to the bit about government and important political figures on Hawking, which was when Eddie spotted two Terran Defense Force soldiers strolling in behind them. She turned to Kierran and found him already looking at her. He was observant, she had to give him that.

They began to walk a bit faster. The soldiers could not possibly be here for Kierran. Not unless Richard had decided to hand him over to the TDF anyway. But if he did that, he would let Eddie know, and as it were, her standing orders were to keep Kierran away from the authorities.

The soldiers did not follow them out of the exhibition area. Eddie cut the guided tour voice short by pulling out her earbud.

Kierran handed her back the one she had coerced him to borrow.

"Well, that was enlightening," she said. Some people craved new information about anything. She kept up with the stuff she cared about. Like the games she played, the music she liked, stuff about spaceships and piloting. That was enough for her unless she specifically needed to learn something for a job.

Richard still had not updated Eddie on the situation. Would it kill him to shoot her a quick message telling her that it would take another hour? If she had known it would take this long, she would have returned to the *Colibri* with Kierran and come back later for Richard.

"Let's get something to eat," Eddie said. By now, she really was hungry. And Kierran ought to be as well. "Any preferences?"

Kierran shook his head.

"You know, as helpful as you might think that is, it's not," Eddie muttered. It wasn't like she had any idea what... Huh. Why not ask an expert? She grinned and pulled up her patch's display.

"Hi," Alannah said when her face appeared on the display. Her expression was mildly worried. "How are things?"

"Fine," Eddie replied. "Or, except—" She cut herself off. It might be a good idea not to go into details. Her patch's security was good, but if the military was involved in this, you never knew. "Richard ran into some of his friends here who turned out to have the same interest, so now he's hanging out with them." She turned so that Kierran's face was in the picture as well. "The two of us are chilling until he gets back. And I was wondering if you have any ideas for a place to grab something to eat here."

Alannah waved at Kierran and then nodded. She was getting the point, all right. "Um... Are you looking for anything special? What's your price range?"

Eddie considered this. "I could go for something fancy. Any high-end restaurant would do."

Alannah raised an eyebrow.

"Richard can cover the expenses later," Eddie explained. She looked over her shoulder at Kierran. They would both look horribly out of place in a fancy restaurant, though. And while she personally enjoyed fucking with other people's preconceptions, they were supposed to not draw any attention to themselves. "But... We probably won't have time for that. I hope," she added. "So something simple would probably do."

"Okay." Alannah looked at a spot next to the display. She probably had another one floating there to look up places. "How about traditional Earth street food? There's a place not too far away from the space observation lounge that specializes in 21st century meals that you can eat on the go. I once had a hot dog there. It was simple, but very tasty."

"A... hot dog?" Eddie asked. That sounded absolutely horrible. And honestly like it should be illegal. And most decidedly not like something animal-loving, idealistic Alannah would ever eat.

"Yes. Oh, it's not actual dog." Alannah grinned. "According to my sources, it used to be dog meat way back, but already in the 21st century, people didn't use meat for it. It's all plant-based."

"Ah. Well, then hot dog it is," Eddie decided.

"I'll send over the directions," Alannah said. "Enjoy your meal and let me know if anything else comes up, okay?"

"Of course. Thanks a bunch." Eddie turned to Kierran as the image of Alannah winked out. "Let's go hunt down a hot dog," she said.

The vendor of said traditional food turned out to have gone out of their way to give the customers an authentic experience. The stall was a small trailer-like contraption plastered with paper posters with pictures of what Eddie assumed were famous people from the 21st century that she didn't recognize. There were an awful lot of pretty, skimpily dressed women, which she didn't mind, and middle-aged white men looking full of themselves, which she did. There was a menu, also printed on paper, next to the window behind which the vendor was preparing food.

Two draevere were waiting for their meal, chatting in Standard with phrases in one of their native languages thrown into the mix.

Eddie studied the menu. There was something called a French hot dog, a plain sausage, plain white bread and then various kinds of garnish for the traditional hot dog.

"What can I get you two?" the vendor asked when it was their turn.

Eddie almost asked Kierran what he wanted, but decided against putting herself through another round of his indifference. "Two hot dogs, please," she said instead.

"With..?" the vendor prompted.

"We've never tried hot dogs before," Eddie told him brightly, "so we're going to trust your judgment."

The vendor smiled. "Do you like pickles?" he asked.

"Yeah," Eddie said.

"No," Kierran said.

Eddie gaped. How did you not like pickles? As if she had needed another reason not to trust him.

"Okay," the vendor said and began his work. He slid a sausage in between two pieces of bread, squeezed some kind of dressing onto the thing, sprinkled roasted onions on top, added pickles to one of the hot dogs and then carefully placed the first one in a contraption that would have looked completely out of place in any other setting. It was a plastic dog, hollow in the middle with only a stylized head wearing a manic grin, legs and a tail. Once the hot dog was placed in it, it became the body of the dog. Then the vendor pressed a sharp metal device onto it, and the hot dog was cut into bite-sized pieces. He carefully scooped it up and placed it inside a wrapper before handing both it and a disposable fork to Eddie. The procedure was then repeated for Kierran.

Eddie paid, grabbed a tissue from the dispenser next to the stall and then beckoned for Kierran to follow her to a bench nearby. "Let's see what all the fuss is about, shall we?" She speared a piece of the hot dog with the fork and put it in her mouth. It was... okay. Not bad, but kind of bland. Eddie was pretty sure spices had been invented by the 21st century. Though, come to think of it, most of the spices she was used to were imported from the cuisines of other species. "What do you think?" she asked Kierran through a mouthful of sausage.

He swallowed a bite, his first. "It appears to have sufficient proteins," he replied.

"But what you you think of the taste?" Eddie insisted.

Kierran frowned. "It's..." He was clearly struggling. "Fine," he finished.

"It's a bit dry. I'll go get us something to drink," Eddie said and handed him her hot dog, deciding there was no point in asking him what he wanted to drink, either. She walked up to the vendor, told him they were enjoying the hot dogs very much, and purchased a couple of soda cans. They were clearly historically inspired too, and the vendor carefully explained how to open them, though it wasn't exactly rocket science.

She turned back and almost stopped in her tracks. Kierran O'Connor, assassin for hire and illegal superhuman soldier was sitting on the bench with a hot dog in each hand, looking more like a puppy whose parents had been turned into hot dog meat than a dangerous killer. So, this was Eddie's life now. Waiting around in space stations, eating weird historic snacks and babysitting murderers. What a glorious career.

As a whole, humanity is part of the interstellar organization known as the Union. Most of us are familiar with a number of other member species, especially our fellow Category 3 species.

As a rule, every planet settled by and space station built by humans are partly self-governed with their own law enforcement and rules, but they are still under the general jurisdiction of our planet of origin, Earth, as evidenced by the presence of the Terran Defense Force and similar institutions. They are also part of the Union and must as such adhere to its rules and regulations like every other species.

However, there are two exceptions worth noting. The first one is the Serenecans which is a strictly pacifist group. They argue that the centralist government of Earth can never take every human settlement's unique needs and interests into consideration because of the vast differences between settlements. They also do not believe that martial powers are necessary, and they feel that the existence of military institutions does not discourage violence and conflict but rather incites it. So they want to cut their ties to the rest of humanity, but they still want to be part of the Union, only recognized as a unique member in their own right.

The other exception is the Olympians. In a way, you can think of their reasons as the exact opposite. They want nothing to do with the Union and are very strict with how many and which people of other species they allow on their planet of settlement, Hestia. Like the Serenecans, they don't want to be under Earth's jurisdiction either, but this is because they want to self-govern in order to exclude other species, have their own military, etc. They still define themselves as humans, and they still want to trade with other human settlements.

Having separationist groups is not unique to humanity. There are similar groups on the political scene of the draevere and the wendek. And you might also have heard of the Utopia Alliance, which is a very interesting project founded by a board of zetois, åayu, draevere and wendek who wanted to create a place where every species would be equal in every possible way. They settled on a planet which wasn't habitable to any of them. That was rather the point as they wanted to form it to suit the needs of all species. By now, quite a few humans have joined the project too.

As a human tourist, you can visit all these places, but it is imperative to read up on local rules and customs.

— Alannah Jackson, *Interstellar Sightseeing 101*

8

ENLIGHTENMENT

Four hours and 16 minutes. That's how long it took before Colonel Dietrich summoned Richard back to their office. By the time he got there, the outer office was empty, and Richard only met one ensign on guard duty on his way through the Force's headquarters. But the door opened as he approached, no doubt because Dietrich kept an eye on surveillance.

"Welcome back, Captain Hart," the Colonel said as he entered. They stood by their desk, looking very much like someone who had been pacing or possibly doing pushups to keep themself alert. Impeccable as always, but with a tired air to them.

"Thank you, Colonel."

"Tea?"

Richard wasn't particularly interested in that. He had been treated to a nostalgically military lunch along with as much black brew and water as he could possibly want, and a bit more, during his stay in and near the military compound. But he decided to accept, if only because the Colonel looked like they needed a strong cup of something or other.

"I take it you are done with Egis, then?" Richard prompted once both of their cups were filled. The tea was lukewarm at this point. Richard wondered how long it had been sitting in the pot.

"As done as I am going to get today," the Colonel said. They sat down and flashed Richard a smile. "It turns out to be an even bigger operation than we theorized."

"Oh?" Richard prompted.

"Some of his testimony was a bit muddled as tends to happen under the influence of aletheia. But Egis has a number of clients who depend on him to send hired killers after someone. A few of them are repeat customers. He has three assassins on hand, though finding out anything about them is even more challenging than sorting out his clients. Obviously, I intend to go after each of them, clients as well as assassins. And I need to act quickly before anyone wonders why they are unable to get in touch with Egis. The only remotely good thing about all this is that Egis has only been on Stonehenge for a very short time."

Richard nodded. It would have looked bad for Dietrich to have Egis running around arranging murders on their watch for years. But now that Egis was here, it clearly was the Colonel's problem. "So, among the clients," Richard said because regardless of the bigger picture, his particular interest was rather personal, "did Egis mention..?"

"Ah." Dietrich blew out their breath in a sigh. "Yes. I know who wants you dead."

"Wonderful. Would you care to enlighten me?" Richard asked when they didn't venture further.

"Egis doesn't know the reason she contracted him, but do you know a woman called Felicia Spencer?" the Colonel asked.

"Felicia Spencer?" Richard echoed. "Yes, I do. Her husband hired me a while back to look into her affairs to determine if she... um, had one, as it were."

"I'm going to assume she did," Dietrich said dryly.

"She did," Richard confirmed, wondering if a joke about them both being prime examples of intelligence officers would be in bad taste. "The husband was strictly monogamous, divorced her and, according to the news, got away with the custody of their child as well as a lot of units." Richard pinched the bridge of his nose with his fingers. "And now... Now she wants me dead because I ruined her marriage?"

"In all fairness," Dietrich said, "she did that herself by not only breaking the rules of a monogamous relationship but also being obvious enough to get caught."

Richard shrugged. "Well, it amounts to the same thing. She hired Egis to get an assassin to dispose of me."

"Yes..." The Colonel leaned back in their chair. "What are we going to do about that?"

"Well, I have a few suggestions," Richard snorted. "I imagine you — Oh. You can't, can you?" He had just realized the one detail about all this that was making it a very difficult case for Dietrich.

Dismay crept over the Colonel's features. "Very astute, Captain. No, I can't. All of Egis' other clients are in areas under Terran Defense Force jurisdiction, but Spencer is located on Hestia. And given her position in the prytaneis, local authorities will alert her if the Force shows up at their doorstep. They would also put up a fight before letting the us take her in. I don't have time to wait for bureaucracy and nepotism, and I'm not letting her get away with this."

"I'm touched," Richard said.

Dietrich managed to contain a smile. "As much as I vastly prefer you alive, it is also on the principle of general justice. And because someone who hires an assassin to take you out is likely to do something like that again."

"Of course," Richard said. "So, what you are saying is that you would prefer to hire an independent party to retrieve her?"

Dietrich arched an eyebrow. "So, what you are saying, Captain Hart, is that you want me to pay you for taking the contractor who arranged for your assassination into custody, after extracting information and giving it to you for free and letting you seek out your quarry like you were intending all along?"

"Well, when you put it like that," Richard muttered. It wasn't his fault Dietrich and their people went after Egis before he even had a chance to.

"I will, however, ask you to bring her here. I have the evidence, and I have the means to interrogate her and make her face justice. Regardless of what the Olympians think of themselves, they are not completely emancipated from the rest of humanity."

"All right," Richard said. It would be the simpler option, anyway.

Dietrich studied him for a moment. "Spencer will probably be surrounded by her own security people. I could lend you an agent."

"Thank you for the offer," Richard said quickly, "but I will manage." He didn't particularly want to turn down the extra help, but he already had O'Connor, and an intelligence officer would notice an enhanced soldier skulking around the *Colibri*. He briefly considered breaking his promise to O'Connor, but it did not feel right. And besides, it was too late now. "Oh, by the way, I completely forgot I had the assassin on board my ship all along, and he happens to be an illegal Terran Defense Force soldier," did not feel like the kind of thing he should admit to the Colonel if he intended them to ever hire him again. No, Richard did intelligence just fine himself, and O'Connor was every bit as efficient in a fight as anyone Dietrich could provide. "I'll be in touch," he said.

"Oh, and Captain," Dietrich added as Richard was getting up to leave. "Keep a lookout for that assassin of yours. He might not know we have Egis. He could try again."

"Yes. Of course," Richard said, making sure not to look too shifty.

Dietrich nodded. If they noticed anything, they didn't say. "One last thing. If you are going to Hestia anyway..."

Alannah had made a batch of black brew and prepared a plate of instant cookies and was waiting for them in the galley when Richard, Eddie and O'Connor returned.

"Just so you know," she said after the initial greetings, "This is not a thing now. I'm not your cook. I was bored waiting for you and procrastinating proof reading."

"So noted," Richard said. Bored as well as worried, he gathered from the nervous energy permeating the air around her.

The snacks had the added bonus of sweetening Eddie's mood as she grabbed a cookie and bit into it. Good. She had been more than usually snarky because of the long wait and not at all happy about being saddled with O'Connor for hours.

"Please help yourself, Kierran," Alannah said, smiling at the enhanced soldier.

Eddie almost didn't scowl.

O'Connor did not take a cookie.

"All right," Richard said after pouring himself a glass of water. He'd had enough liquid caffeine for one day. "When we arrived on Stonehenge, a group of Terran Defense Force officers had made it ahead of us and were arresting Egis," he said for Alannah's benefit. "It turns out my, um, contact there was onto him already."

"Your contact being the mysterious Colonel, I assume?" Eddie asked.

"Yes, the very same. I had to wait for them to interrogate Egis before I could meet up with you again."

"When you say interrogate," Alannah prompted, "what does that entail?"

"Not tearing off anyone's fingernails," Richard replied. "The Colonel did a pharmaceutically assisted interrogation. Anyway, they mean to look into and go after anyone who contracted Egis in the past as well as locate and catch his hired killers."

Richard caught a narrowing of O'Connor's eyes and a stiffening of his posture, but the young soldier said nothing.

—

80

"I honored our agreement," Richard told him. "As far as anyone not present at this table is concerned, you escaped after failing to kill me on Dwebl."

"Thank you," Kierran said.

"Okay, but if your Colonel is going after literally everyone else," Eddie said, "then what do we do? Call it a day and move on?"

"Not quite," Richard said, not adding that he wished Eddie would stop calling Dietrich his Colonel. It would only make her do it on purpose to annoy him. "They told me who contracted Egis to contract O'Connor. It turns out to be a woman whose husband hired me to spy on her to confirm or debunk his suspicion that she had an affair with someone else. It turned out he was absolutely correct. There was a messy divorce and apparently, that was enough for her to want revenge on me."

"When was this?" Eddie asked.

"A month or two before I hired you," Richard said.

"Ah." Eddie nodded sagely. "Of course. See, this kind of thing would never have happened with me on board."

"That," Richard said, pointing a finger at her, "makes absolutely no sense at all."

Eddie shrugged. "So this cheating psycho bitch sent a killer after you because you bruised her ego," she summed it up and flicked a glance at Alannah. She brought up her hands in defense. "Hey, don't look at me like that. You'd have to be a psycho bitch to hire an assassin, end of story. I'm not going to sugar-coat that just because there's a professional murderer with big blue puppy eyes on my ship."

"My ship," Richard reminded her. "Anyway, the Force is letting me go after her."

"You mean, they are making you do their dirty work?" Eddie snorted.

Why was it that everyone he employed seemed to want to antagonize the military? The only reason Richard wasn't an officer anymore was his early retirement. "Not quite," he said. "The... psycho bitch in question is a member of the prytaneis on Hestia."

"Oh," Alannah said. "That makes sense, then."

"The who?" Eddie asked.

Richard made an encouraging gesture at Alannah.

"For the past few years," she began, slipping straight into tourist guide mode, "a separationist group called the Olympians has attempted to declare independence from the Union. But they still want to enjoy the same benefits as all other human settlements and stations. And given the resources in the Hestia system, the rest of humanity has an interest in keeping them in the shipyard, so to speak. So there is a huge legal tug-o-war going on."

"Well, yes, I knew about all that" Eddie said, "but I imagine Richard's Colonel could just go in and make some demands, couldn't they?"

"See, that brings us to the prytaneis. They are the governing body on Hestia, and they are basically an oligarchy made up of very rich people. That's the problem, right?" Alannah said, verbally flying the chick back into Richard's nest.

"It is," he said. "As part of the prytaneis, Spencer personally funds a large part of Hestia. Dietrich assures me that if they did this officially, there would be so many delays and investigations that she might vanish or get so much media attention that other clients of Egis would be alerted. If I apprehend her and drag her to Stonehenge, however, they just happen to have enough proof to interrogate her and put her on trial."

Eddie crossed her arms over her chest. "Okay," she said, "but please enlighten me as to how that is not making you do the dirty work. Oh, are they paying us?"

Richard drummed his fingers on the table. "No," he admitted. "Since I am an independent party, they consider trading me her identity and location enough. And since my plan was to go after her anyway..." He cleared his throat. "On that note, I am going to need your assistance, O'Connor. Spencer is likely to have substantial security. As for the rest of you..."

"Here we go," Eddie said and threw her hands in the air. "We can leave it to the soldier boys! This is Richard's problem and not ours! He'll go be a hero with the hitman, manly men doing masculine things, and maybe we can catch up on our sandwich-making skills in the meantime."

Richard glared at her. "That," he said, "is not what I'm implying. I don't give a damn what's in your pants. But yes, it is my problem."

"Cute," Eddie said. "Obviously, I'm going with you. How many times are we going to have this conversation?"

Alannah coughed. "I will go if you have a job for me," she said.

"As it happens, I think I do," Richard said.

"Whoa, hey!" Eddie interrupted. "You don't mean to put Alannah in danger? You can't do that!"

"What, do you think I should practice my sandwich-making skills?" Alannah asked prudently.

"Please," Richard groaned, "will you all just listen to me?"

It was the invasive regulations and policies that ultimately convinced the Olympians to break away from the Union. It is a scary thought indeed that a board of aliens, many of them representing races that do not resemble humans in the least and who could not possibly begin to understand, let alone protect, our needs and interests, should decide how we govern our own worlds and stations.

A prime example of the effects of this alien meddling is the Terran Defense Force. If the restrictions suddenly imposed upon humanity's guard against intruders and aggressors are devised by the very same aliens against whom we might one day see it necessary to defend ourselves, what use is it even for that military institution to exist?

We live in an age when our children get their ideas of good and evil from superficial and biased wendek entertainment. They are coerced to learn a language not designed with any of Earth's native tongues in mind, even on Earth itself. Elementary education focuses more on zetoi and åayu history and religion than that of our own heritage. And we are supposed to be best friends with the very same draevere who time and again challenge and threaten our ways.

When the Olympians colonized (or "settled on" as the currently politically correct term goes) Hestia, it was with the intent to provide humanity with an unpolluted, authentic sanctuary to call home. It was to ensure that our children can grow up safely regardless of what one alien force or another may decree.

On Hestia, you will not find unsavory draever restaurants or neighborhoods catering to the strange, amphibian needs of åayu. You will not find vertical, insurmountable buildings that only zetoi can access or wendek venues denying anyone with the slightest body odor access.

In short, the Olympians seek to protect humanity by putting some distance between ourselves and the so-called interstellar community (a quaint name; communities are by definition smaller groups with the same interests!). Even if the rest of humanity seems to have forgotten, we are humans first and foremost.

— Sophia Calimeris, excerpt from article on VoidNet

9
CEREAL KILLER

Courier ships usually had at least two pilots on board to be able to switch between them. This made sense because they literally made their living by jumping quickly from one station to the next every day. The same was the case for freight ships, although their trips were usually longer and with breaks to pick up cargo. In her Trans World Trading days, Eddie usually had or was a co-pilot, and on long hauls, they would take turns because even pilots hopped up on hyper had to sleep sometimes. In the beginning, that had been all there was to it. Then came all the restrictions and rules concerning hyper. Eddie only learned how used to regular doses she was when forced to take a holiday which was, ironically, mandatory as not to get pilots addicted to hyper.

Richard only employed one pilot, but he was a law-abiding citizen of the interstellar community when it came to Eddie's hyper use. And so, it wasn't until the following day that the *Colibri* was scheduled to sail out of the Stonehenge docks.

Eddie poured a steaming mug of black brew, handed it to Alannah, poured another for herself and paused, wondering why

Richard wasn't in the galley yet. The thing about the *Colibri* was that it felt like family. Or like family should feel, maybe. The ship was home. Richard was the nagging, slightly over-protective know-it-all older brother. Eddie was the rebellious but loyal kid sister. And after Alannah joined… Well, she didn't feel like a sister to Eddie, but Eddie liked the shape of Alannah in this flying home of theirs on so many levels.

"Good morning," Richard said as he entered the galley.

"Good morning," Alannah trilled. "Slept well?"

And then there was the super soldier trailing after Richard. He had been locked up over night. Oh yeah. He certainly did not feel like family.

Eddie poured a cup for Richard and handed it to him.

"Thanks, Eddie," he said and made his way to the table.

Eddie and Kierran stood looking at each other for a moment. "Do you want black brew or not?" Eddie asked.

Kierran's pale brows knitted briefly as if she had fielded a completely unexpected question. His eyes darted to Alannah for help, but her back was turned. "Yes. Thank you," he said, clearly forgetting not to be monosyllabic in his confusion.

"See, that wasn't so hard," Eddie murmured and poured him a cup. "Help yourself to breakfast, I guess."

"We don't have anything fancy," Alannah chirped in and gestured for Kierran to join her at the cupboard next to the fridge. "What do you usually have for breakfast?"

Eddie tuned out his reply. "When do you want to jump?" she asked Richard.

"In an hour," he replied after glancing at his patch. "I want everybody to have time to eat their breakfast and get ready."

"It's not a five course meal," Eddie said. "How long can it take to eat a bowl of Crunchy Asteroids?"

"Are you in a hurry?" Richard asked. "Not withdrawal already, right?"

"No, of course not!" Eddie told him indignantly. She wasn't getting jittery from lack of hyper after one day.

Alannah and Kierran joined them at the table. Alannah's shoulder touched Eddie's in a comfortable way as she slid onto the seat next to her. Kierran sat down next to Richard, not touching. He frowned at the bowl of pink and blue clumps of cereal as if he had never seen the stuff before. He picked up the spoon and experimentally dipped it.

"You're super good at eating cereal," was not a compliment Eddie had ever given anyone, and she was not about to. She hadn't previously considered it a life skill. But the soldier looked so totally out of place and so completely unused to operating a spoon that she couldn't stand looking at it. She had assumed the awkwardness with the hot dog was because it was a weird kind of food, but... Sentiments violently at odds crashed into each other in her brain. She wanted to laugh at him, but at the same time, she had been the underdog enough times in her life to recognize another and take pity when she saw them. But then again, she could not possibly think of a fucking murderer as anything like herself. "I'll get the *Colibri* ready," she said and stood up.

Eddie's multidirectional anger dissipated the moment she got to the cockpit. It was her favorite place on the *Colibri*. She belonged there.

She opened the safe and took out a dose of hyper. Placed it within reach of the pilot's seat and slid on a headset so she could communicate with the ship without having to deal with Richard's habit of muting whatever could be muted. A quick sweep of her fingers brought the controls in front of her to life. Once in a while, when she couldn't sleep, Eddie would go up here and just sit wrapped in a blanket, staring out at the displayed portion of space in front of her until her brain was lulled into some kind of comfort. Usually she went back to bed after that, but once she had fallen asleep so thoroughly that she only woke up when Richard found her and demanded to know what she was doing.

———

88

Eddie went through the motions with station control and let the *Colibri* glide away from Stonehenge, following the route she was given.

"Hi," Richard said as he slipped into the co-pilot's seat.

"Did you lock him up again?" Eddie asked.

"No," Richard replied.

"So he's just going to run around the ship now?" she asked.

"He's not running around. He's sensibly seated waiting for you to jump, just like Alannah and me."

Eddie shook her head. "I don't like it."

"You don't have to," Richard replied.

Eddie injected the hyper into her connector and began her pre-jump checks. All systems looking good. She tapped the alert for everyone on board so they knew she was about to jump, a new procedure for Alannah's benefit. And hyper surged to her head in a whirlwind that momentarily erased all her complaints about assassins and, well, everything else that she could possibly complain about. Richard's presence and her own physical shape faded into the background, and her eyes and her mind were on the stars.

It was a smooth jump, and an equally smooth ride. Hyperspace was behaving nicely today. She coasted on hyperwind, putting light years between herself and the Hawking system in moments. And although the trip took several subjective hours for her, it also felt like hardly any time had passed at all when she emerged back into the slowness of normal space.

Eddie tapped the display again to signal that the *Colibri* was out of hyperspace, although probably everybody would have noticed on their own. She sighed and leaned back in her seat. Just one moment of absolute, content peace.

Next to her, Richard was checking their coordinates as if she would accidentally take them to the wrong place.

"Welcome to the Hestia system," Eddie said in that weird slow motion way she had to speak when hyper was coursing through her body.

Outside the *Colibri*, Rheia Station was suspended in orbit around Hestia. From this distance, it could be any human station and planet. There was nothing about it that screamed separationist space.

"Have you been to Hestia before?" Richard asked.

Eddie nudged the *Colibri* forward, unbearably slowly. "No," she said. "I once piloted a cargo ship to Rheia, but didn't even get to see the station. You?"

"Apart from that one job I clearly shouldn't have taken on, no," Richard sighed.

"Ah," Eddie said. Station control greeted her, first in a language she didn't understand, and then in English. No Standard, but that wasn't a great surprise. There was a bit more back and forth between her and the person on the other end of the connection than she was used to, which wasn't surprising, either.

"And now that we have established we aren't smuggling a draever onto their precious little planet..." she muttered to herself.

"Come again?" Richard said. "Anything I need to know?"

"No," she replied as she began to approach the spot where station control had directed her to park the ship. "I told them we aren't bringing any aliens. Should I have told them we have an illegal enhanced soldier on board, though?"

"Probably best to skip that part," Richard said.

"Thought so." Eddie found the spot and coasted into place.

A short while later, Eddie, Richard and Kierran were on their way to Hestia in the *Colibri*'s chick. Alannah was going there too, but she had taken a public transport instead. The official story was that she was going as a travel guide writer, and they were visiting friends. Eddie was glad that Alannah's part of this job was a low-risk one. Not that Eddie herself would be in any real danger, either. In fact, it was a bit annoying that Richard had opted for bringing Kierran to the more precarious task.

They landed in a small chick port outside the city of Oikos, on the opposite side of the more busy commercial port where Alannah was going. This was a lot more discreet, and also much closer to the location where their quarry lived. All the other chicks there were new and shiny, most of them bigger than the one Eddie was setting down. Except a very sleek model with room for no more than two people that she would have liked to take for a spin. She wondered if that belonged to Spencer. She also wondered if perhaps there was any reason to take it into custody so she could try flying it. But sadly, breaking into and stealing a chick wasn't on their itinerary.

"All right," Richard said when they were all standing outside the chick, armed and equipped with everything they might need, and then some. Richard did love his gadgets. "Any questions?"

Kierran shook his head.

Eddie made a mock salute. "Nope," she said. "Time to get out of the nest."

Richard's gaze swept over them. One final inspection. "Let's move out," he said.

Emerging from HS near Rheia Station. Looks like any other human-built station, but not as heavy traffic as Stonehenge, Yellowstone, etc. ONLY human ship designs in sight!

Eddie: station control is polite, but more questions about purpose/length of visit than other human stations. Emphasis on whether we are bringing any "aliens".

NB: Just spotted one åayu ship about to dock. (makes sense with the åayu being the friendliest/most peaceful species ever)

Hestia looks like most planetformed/naturally human-friendly planets from space. Two moons. (remember: stats on population numbers, main cities, climate, indigenous plants and animals)

Getting through the chick port in the outskirts of Oikos City. Not as much security as expected.

First impressions: typical for a settlement's first/biggest city. Port once center of city, strict layout of streets/utilitarian architecture. Newer parts more organic/constructed with local materials.

No street signs in Standard! Only English/Greek.

Add mythological/historical info on Olympians/Hestia/the prytaneis later!

— Alannah Jackson's travel notes

10
FAVORS

Alannah glanced at the piece of dead tree in her hand. Richard's mysterious Colonel must be quite the character to insist on writing letters on paper and having random people going to the recipient's location deliver them. To Alannah's regret, the envelope was not closed with a wax seal. It had a neat little strip that needed to be torn off in order to open it. Not that she would be tempted to pry open any kind of seal. It would just have completed the archaic picture.

In any case, Alannah was glad to be useful on this mission, even if her usefulness stretched only as far as handing a message from one Terran Defense Force officer to another. Or, she assumed the person she was going to find was a military officer. She had only been given a first name.

She stopped at an intersection and inspected the signs above the road. Like in most settlements, they were in two languages. Uniquely for Hestia, none of them were in Standard, but Greek and English respectively. Hestia's majority wasn't actually made up of people with Greek heritage, but it was the Olympians' language of choice. Alannah assumed there must be a culturally relevant reason on some level, but from what she had been able to learn about the people here, it seemed like they had dug deep into the historical recesses of the human consciousness and decided that associating everything on Hestia with Ancient Greek myths was the way to go.

A car went by with a low hum. Aside from the language choices, Oikos looked like a typical first city with a commercial chick port in the figurative backyard of what was once the geographical city center. Now it hung back while increasingly organic and unplanned neighborhoods sprang up.

What was different was the lack of any variety in population as well as remarkably few tourists. The first was deliberate, of course. The whole idea of the settlers on this planet was to distance themselves from the Union, so very few, if any, members of other species were allowed permanent residency. The latter was a direct consequence of the general hostility to outsiders.

Alannah crossed the street and entered the cafe she was supposed to go to. It, too, looked like any other human cafe. A couple of people were seated at tables, talking over the local variety of black brew or tea. Music was playing softly, a generic kind of song that Alannah couldn't pinpoint. It, too, may be local.

At a first glance, it looked like there was no one serving the patrons. Alannah still approached the counter. A menu was displayed above it, also in Greek and English, alternating between clips of various kinds of beverages being poured into cups and glasses. Ice cubes clinking together, steaming black brew, different kinds of foam and toppings... They all looked very delicious and made Alannah want to sample the selection.

A young man suddenly popped up from behind the counter. He was smiling brightly and said something in Greek.

She almost jumped back. "Yiasou," she greeted him, which was about 20% of her total usable Greek vocabulary. She felt inappropriately embarrassed about that, but she had never had any reason to learn Greek. "Do you speak English?"

"Yes, I do," the young man replied. He was probably around Kierran's age, but taller and lankier. His skin was light brown, and he had a mob of dark, curly hair tied into a short ponytail. He was wearing a white shirt and a dark blue apron with a name tag saying Julien and the same, Alannah assumed, in the Greek alphabet. "What can I get you?"

"I'm looking for Cora," Alannah said.

"Ah," the barista said, flashing her a charming smile. "That's my boss. But she's not here. Are you a friend of hers?"

"We're not close," Alannah said, which was true, except it gave the wrong impression she was an acquaintance. "I'm really just here to deliver a letter to her."

"Oh?" Julien cocked his head inquisitively.

"It's from a friend of hers. Another friend asked me to give her the letter," Alannah explained and held it up.

The barista's eyes widened as he took in the paper envelope. Then he schooled his expression, but there had been recognition as well as surprise on his face. Alannah was certain of that.

"What's her friend's name?" he asked.

"Micah," Alannah said, which was how Richard had instructed her to speak of the Colonel in case they came up in conversation.

"Ah, I thought so," the barista said. "Well, I know Micah too. You can give me the letter."

Alannah narrowed her eyes. "But it's not for you."

"No," he said, "But I work for her." Emphasis on the work and the preposition and a meaningful glance. "And there is more than a kernel of truth in that," he added.

Okay, that one was pretty clever if it was a clue and not just a local expression. Alannah studied him for a moment.

"Sure, a black brew!" the barista exclaimed as if replying to something Alannah had said. "Do you want milk or sweetener in that?"

"Milk, please," Alannah said automatically, wondering what the hell was going on here.

"Soy or local?"

"Local, please," Alannah replied because it was always best to appear open to new variations of milk.

"Just one moment." The barista turned away from her to make the black brew.

Alannah studied him. There wasn't anything about this young man that suggested he was a secret operative from the Terran Defense Force's intelligence branch. She could not for the life of her picture the barista in a military uniform. But then, that might be the whole point. She compared him to the one intelligence officer she knew or, well, former intelligence officer. Richard Hart had more of a soldier-bearing about him. Alannah could easily picture him in a uniform.

"Here you go," the barista said and handed the large cup over the counter. "I hope you like it."

"Thanks," Alannah said. "How many units?"

"On the house. You can drink it while I read the letter," the barista suggested, still smiling his winning smile at her.

"But—" Alannah began. Then she looked down. The foamy milk on top of her black brew had not been whipped or poured into a heart or a star or the logo of the cafe. No, the barista had written out a message in tiny letters.

I am TDF, it said.

Alannah looked back up at the barista. He was wiping down the counter now, inconspicuously. This probably counted as proof that she could hand over the letter to him, right? She held out the envelope.

"Thank you," he said and took it. "Enjoy your black brew."

"Thanks," Alannah said and made her way to one of the many free tables. She took a careful sip of the hot beverage. It tasted... Well, it tasted pretty much like a variation of black brew on any other human station or planet. She tapped her forefinger on the table. It would be a while before the others were done with their job. She might as well use the opportunity to do some sightseeing and take a few more notes. There weren't many travel guides to Hestia around, for obvious reasons. And sure, the market for them wasn't great, but Alannah could still write something about the place. If nothing else, it would provide interesting material to compare with other settlements.

She pulled up a blank document and a keyboard on her patch and began to write down her thoughts.

"Hey," said a voice after Alannah was halfway through her cup of black brew and a few hundred words into her collection of thoughts on Oikos.

She looked up at the barista. "Yes?"

He smiled, and Alannah realized he wasn't wearing his apron anymore. A quick glance at the counter told her someone else was there now. "Since my boss isn't here at the moment," he continued, "I thought I could keep you company for a bit, if you don't mind."

"Um..." Alannah cleared her throat. She was usually good at deciphering when someone was flirting with her, and there was nothing about this young man that suggested he was. Sure, he wore that bright, friendly smile, but it was just that. Friendly.

"I mean, unless there is a strict reason you want her?"

"I only needed to hand over the letter," Alannah said with a shrug.

"And I'm making sure she gets it, of course," the barista said. "But she isn't coming back for a while, and I have the rest of the day off." He stressed the last word oddly, as if there were some quotation marks involved. As if Alannah ought to get an inside joke, which she didn't.

"Well, I was going to take a stroll around the city. See the sights and the people. Take a few notes. I write travel guides," she added by way of explanation. "But I'm not staying for long."

The barista grinned at her and nodded knowingly. "All the more reason to get the most out of it, then. I'll show you around. You aren't fluent in Greek, right?"

It seemed to be a legit question. "No," she admitted. But in addition to all the English signs, she also did have a translator on her patch, even if it was a bit awkward to use.

"I think a native guide is in order, then. Greek is predominant in some parts of town, and I would hate for you to miss out."

Alannah thought for a moment, but she could see no reason why she shouldn't take the barista up on his offer. She smiled and held out her hand. "Thank you. I'm Alannah, by the way."

He shook her hand. "I'm Julien, like it said on the tag. Nice to meet you!"

EXT. EMPTY STREET - NIGHT

WORRA (checking her weapons, reveals several dart guns inside her coat. She is also wearing nose plugs.)
Ready for some action?

DARITH (crunches a Crack-Shot between their teeth, winks at Worra. They too are wearing nose plugs, though they don't fit tightly due to their piercings.)
Always.

Worra nods at them and kicks open the backdoor.

INT. THE BAR - DIM LIGHT, CLOUDS OF DRUG VAPOR OBSCURING THE VIEW

NOLYETH (surprised and angry.)
What the thak?

DARITH (aiming their signature EMP gun at him)
Surprised to see us, old man?

Nolyeth dives behind the bar and reaches for his own firearm. Several patrons scream, duck under tables or stampede toward the front door. Firefight ensues. Darith leaps onto a table to get a clean shot but has to dodge a kinetic projectile from Nolyeth's gun.

WORRA (eyes widening as she spots five of Nolyeth's hench people all aiming at Darith)
Watch out!

Darith somersaults off the table in their trademark style, firing multiple rapid shots at the hench people. Two of them drop, twitching.

Worra tackles Darith when they land, throwing them both to the floor. A shot narrowly misses Darith.

DARITH
Hey there.

WORRA
Please try not to get yourself shot this time?

DARITH
Isn't that what I have you for, babe?

WORRA
Just try to keep up, you dimdek.

Worra rolls off Darith, jumps to her feet and launches herself at Nolyeth, kicking the gun out of his hand. She wrestles him into a choke hold and aims her weapon at his head.

WORRA
Everybody drops their weapon now! Or I will shoot your boss!

The hench people hesitate, but one of them has moved into Worra's blind spot and is about to take a shot at her.
Darith, still on their knees, quickly drops the hench person with a single shot.

WORRA
Anyone else?

The remaining hench people put their weapons down and raise their hands in surrender.

WORRA
I thought so. Looks like we have quite a catch for the Superior Investigations Chief today.

DARITH (grinning at her)
You're welcome.

NOLYETH (defeated)
Why are you two always poking your noses in my affairs?

WORRA (wrinkles her nose in disgust)
Trust me when I say your affairs is the last thing we want our noses in.

DARITH (breathes in deeply through their ill-fitting nose plugs, makes a face)
Speaking of which... We'd better get out of here before the vapors get too bad.

— Excerpt from *Worra & Darith* season 4, episode 7, *A Study in Pink and Perfumes*

11
ABDUCTION 101

The worst problem with this job was that it felt more like being a vigilante than a private investigator. On a normal job, Richard would have an employer and be solving a case based on an agreed upon contract. But right now, he was his own employer, at least partly. The other employer was Micah Dietrich who paid nothing for his services. And then there was the fact that he was bringing along Kierran O'Connor. Richard was still convinced the plan had its merits. But the enhanced assassin was a wildcard, a calculated risk.

"What did you say they were paying you for killing Richard?" Eddie asked O'Connor.

"50,000 units," O'Connor said.

"Hm." Eddie tapped her lips with her forefinger. "I feel like someone who lives in a place like that ought to be able to fork over a bit more."

O'Connor shrugged. "Egis took part of the salary."

Richard cleared his throat. "Are you two done discussing how much my life is worth?" he asked.

Eddie grinned. "Not entirely. You mind?"

Richard sighed. He knew why she was doing this. It was her way of dealing with stress, but still. "There's a time and a place, Eddie. We need to get moving."

The residence of Felicia Spencer was sprawling on the lawn in front of them, and it was no modest estate. It looked like it was modeled on, or at least inspired by, some kind of grand, old Earth architecture. Richard wanted to say something from the ancient Greek empire, but probably not everything with columns and elaborate frescoes was Greek. The general idea of this place was obvious, though. Huge, white and grand. And it was guarded well. In the time the three of them had been observing the premises, Richard had tracked the movements of the guards in dark blue uniforms outside the building, and it should be possible to slip past them without any complications. But there would undoubtedly be guards inside too.

"Let's go over the plan again," Richard said.

Eddie groaned.

O'Connor's eyebrows drew down in a scowl. Richard, irrationally, felt like telling him this wasn't the military and that there was no problem with his way of commanding. He didn't.

"Eddie, I want you on the outside so you can notify us of any irregularities in the sentries' activities and alert us," Richard continued. "O'Connor, you are with me. We slip in, find our target and retrieve her. After that, we notify Alannah, retreat directly to the chick, and fly back to the *Colibri*. Any questions?"

"No," O'Connor said, wonderfully promptly.

"No, sir," Eddie supplied, sounding immensely bored.

Richard assessed them both for a moment. "All right," he said. "Let's move."

They left Eddie hidden from view and out of danger behind some trees and shrubbery on the hill that overlooked the estate. She hadn't complained about this task. Richard had half expected her to go on about how he should bring her instead of O'Connor, but he was glad that she saw reason. She wasn't half bad in a combat situation, but

Richard had to admit that bringing a soldier with superhuman combat abilities was preferable to any civilian. Even if that soldier happened to have attempted to assassinate Richard.

Taking point, Richard pulled up the facemask dangling around his neck and jogged in a half circle around the building to the location with the least exposure for the least amount of time according to his calculations. Security was always tighter at main entrances, despite the fact that anyone trying to get in covertly would probably opt for another route.

He stopped and looked over his shoulder to check that O'Connor was where he was supposed to be. The enhanced moved uncannily silently. But yes, he was right at Richard's heels, looking the cat burglar part in his own mask and black clothes.

Richard set off toward the house, running fast and ready to drop and roll in case a sentry should appear. But they made it to the house unhindered. Richard retrieved a rope from his backpack, tossed it to O'Connor and linked his fingers, bracing himself.

O'Connor stepped into his hands, and Richard thrust upward, boosting the younger soldier up the vertical wall of the building. O'Connor found purchase quickly and pulled himself up by the gutter to the place where the slanting roof met the wall. He looped one end of the rope around an ornamental figure and threw the other end down to Richard, then sat down with his feet braced against the ornament for leverage.

Richard took hold of the rope and began to rappel up the wall. He was scrambling up next to O'Connor in hardly any time. While the enhanced unfastened the rope and stuffed it back into the backpack, Richard scanned their surroundings. No one had noticed them. But this was the easy part of the job.

They continued upward, staying low as not to stand out to anyone keeping an eye on the premises from the ground, and reached a window set almost at the crest of the roof. It was alarmed, of course. But there was a neat trick to disabling that feature. Richard pulled out a shocker from one of the weapon holsters he was wearing. O'Connor flinched, the first time Richard had seen him do anything of the sort. He automatically filed the knowledge for later.

Richard adjusted the setting on the shocker to calibrate it for this kind of job. He held it as close to the window as he could without direct contact and squeezed the trigger. The small light blinking inside flickered and went out. He holstered the shocker again and took out another handy gadget to quickly disable the lock and pry open the window. So far, the plan was going without a hitch. Richard liked when plans did that. When a simple retrieval mission didn't turn into an assassination attempt, for instance. He gestured for the aforementioned assassin to lead, and O'Connor slid through the window and landed on the floor as silently as a prowling syraxh. He unholstered a dart gun and, scanning the room, nodded for Richard to follow.

Being taller and all around bulkier than O'Connor, Richard's own descent was not as graceful, but he landed on his feet well enough.

The room was a storage space as Richard had hoped. Empty but for crates and boxes and what looked like a statue shrouded in white fabric.

Richard put on a visor and switched to an overlay that would make it easier to avoid meeting anyone they didn't want to meet, which was pretty much anyone except their target. O'Connor did not have a visor and had declined the offer to borrow one. His inorganic eye was upgraded with everything Richard's equipment could offer and, Richard suspected, probably more as well. He felt the urge to reiterate his order to keep any kind of violence to an absolute minimum, but he had provided O'Connor with a weapon and knew which darts were loaded in it.

Before leaving the *Colibri*, Eddie had asked him what kept the enhanced from just turning the dart gun on Richard and presenting him to the woman who wanted him dead. It was a valid question because nothing truly did. But Richard was sure he had the hired killer figured out. Egis had effectively been taken out of the equation and Spencer had no idea who O'Connor was. Even if she found out, she probably didn't want to interact directly with him. She might be a member of the prytaneis, but it would take more than that to avoid investigation if she convinced one home intruder to kill another.

Richard took point again as they left the storage room and began to make their way through the hallway outside. They were the only people on this level of the building. Opting for the back staircase instead of an elevator, the former soldiers quickly found themselves on the level below. Here, there were two other people. One was stationary inside a room. The other was moving at a steady pace.

O'Connor followed Richard through the house. If any of them had been into art appreciation or cared about interior decoration, they might have paid more attention to their surroundings, but Richard's focus was honed in on the mission and nothing else. When he did notice a statue in an alcove as they crept by, it was not the artistic execution or the monetary value he paid attention to. It was the way a person could slip into the shadows and hide there. The way the statue could be toppled over to create confusion or block a pursuer's path.

Avoiding the other person moving about was simple enough. Before long, they reached the door of the room where their target was. Or where they hoped she was.

Richard positioned himself on one side of the door, dart gun at the ready. He gave O'Connor a nod, and the enhanced soldier landed a swift kick on the door. As it flew open, Richard swept in, spotted the target and fired. After all, this wasn't an episode of *Worra & Darith*. In entertainment, people always jeoparized their own job by talking. In real life, efficiency was so much more important.

Felicia Spencer was standing by a desk, studying the display floating between the rods. She didn't look very different from last time Richard saw her. Well, except she was clothed right now and not straddling an equally naked man who was not her husband.

Her head snapped up, and her hand went to the side of her neck where Richard's dart had already lodged itself. Her eyes widened, and she reached out for something on the desk with the other hand.

Richard dashed for her, managing to take hold of her arm as she collapsed. He didn't particularly care about the welfare of someone who had sent an assassin after him, but it could complicate things if she injured her head going down. Even a few harmless bruises were preferable to avoid. He didn't want to have to explain to Colonel Dietrich or anyone else that he had not abused the target.

He looked up at O'Connor. The young man had placed himself by the door, ready to intercept anyone who approached them.

Richard pried open the strap of the patch on Spencer's wrist and tossed it on the floor. There were plenty of other ways to verify her identity, and a patch would be too easy to track. It was better not to leave behind any traces for now. Better to get off the planet before anyone started searching for them. That was abduction 101.

He arranged the limp form on his shoulder, much like he had carried O'Connor off Dwebl only a couple of days ago. Spencer was lighter, unsurprisingly. O'Connor was pure muscle and metal, after all. He was also taking point on the way back down the corridor and up the staircase. By the time they reached the window they had entered through, Richard was breathing hard, wondering how wendek managed to look so comfortable in the masks they wore. His hands were slippery with sweat inside his gloves, and his legs felt like he had run a marathon. Richard decided all this was due to the unhandy extra weight and not a sign that he was out of shape or getting older. After all, getting in was always so much easier than getting out.

O'Connor effortlessly leapt onto the edge of the window, looked out and then back at Richard. He gestured for Richard to hand over the unconscious woman.

Richard shifted the not-literal dead weight and lifted her up to O'Connor who deftly got her out. Once Richard was out too, he motioned for O'Connor to give back their abductee.

O'Connor pulled down his mask enough for Richard to see his mouth. "It's faster if I carry her," he said, matter of factly.

Richard had to admit it was a valid point. "Agreed," he said and fastened the rope once more. He rappelled back down with no problems, then kept watch while O'Connor did the same. The enhanced soldier only got halfway before jumping the rest of the way. He landed perfectly balanced and still holding Spencer with one hand.

Richard quickly checked his patch. Nothing from Eddie. Good. That meant they could slip out of here without any complications. Who would have thought it was actually going to be this easy?

Now, Richard Hart was not superstitious. He had known soldiers who were, despite their training and otherwise logical mindsets. They carried charms for luck or performed rituals before a mission. Richard had routines too, but he didn't believe they did anything supernatural. They only honed his resolve and focus. This was why he didn't jump to the conclusion that he had jinxed the whole affair when, seconds after considering how smooth things were going, someone shouted behind them.

Given the context, he didn't need a proper connection between his ears and brain to figure out what they were shouting about. He turned, bringing up his dart gun.

A loud crack pierced the air, and pain exploded in Richard's right arm. His teeth clamped shut on a scream. That was no dart gun or EMP gun. In a way, that was preferable right now as a kinetic projectile would not immediately take him out unless it hit a vital spot. Still, he was struggling to keep his breathing somewhat even, and the white-hot agony made his arm practically useless.

As Richard turned, he saw a total of three people tearing after them. Two of them wore the dark blue uniform of Spencer's private guards. The last one, ahead of them by a few paces, wore a business suit. Richard was fairly sure she was the one who had hit him. Trying to compartmentalize his burning arm somewhere at the very back of his mind, he aimed a left-handed shot at her.

O'Connor was saying something as he appeared by Richard's side holding onto his burden with his artificial hand and aiming his dart gun at the party pursuing them with the other.

"Take them out," Richard told him.

His own dart had found its target well enough, but the woman in the suit must be wearing protection under her clothes because she was not slowing down. He gritted his teeth and fired again, this time aiming for her exposed throat. Another projectile whizzed past him, but finally the woman staggered and toppled over.

O'Connor fired twice, taking out the two other guards in rapid succession. One of them managed to fire back before they crumpled, but the shot went completely astray.

"Go!" Richard ordered. He glanced at his patch, ignoring the fact that his sleeve was rapidly getting soaked with blood. Still nothing from Eddie. But she must have noticed the kinetic gunshots from her vantage point.

They ran up the slope, zigzagging in between trees, and back to the rendezvous point. And... There was no sign of Eddie.

Richard whipped around, panting, bleeding, sweating, hurting and extremely annoyed that Eddie hadn't stayed where he had told her to. What the hell was she doing?

O'Connor said something.

"What?" Richard snapped.

O'Connor pointed at the ground with his gun.

And Richard realized what he was getting at. Damnit. The grass and scrubs were trampled, and the ground bore marks from more than Eddie's vigil here. Someone else had been here and from the broken flower stems and branches, it looked very much like there had a been a struggle. Which meant... Richard's knees wanted to buckle. What if they had killed her... No. No, it made more sense to take her in for questioning. Richard took a few deep breaths. "I need to find her," he said. "You can fly a chick, right? Go back to the *Colibri*."

O'Connor pulled down his mask. "No," he said.

Richard glared at him and, as a precaution, swung up his gun to point it at him.

"If your pilot was apprehended, she is likely to be in the custody of Spencer's security people," O'Connor continued calmly and completely unwinded. "You are injured and stand little chance of retrieving her on your own."

"I am not leaving her behind!" Richard told him. Warm blood was seeping into his glove by now.

"No, you are leaving me here," O'Connor said. "I will find and retrieve her while you go back to the ship with Spencer. It is the most logical option."

Richard lowered his gun. There was nothing logical about trusting the man who had tried to murder him only a few days ago with saving Eddie. But he had counted on O'Connor so far and it was still the option that stood the best chance of success. "If you fail," he said, "I am willing to use Spencer as a hostage to be exchanged."

"Understood." O'Connor unceremoniously removed Spencer from his person to arrange her on Richard's uninjured side.

"Keep me informed," Richard said, or rather gasped as he tried to hold on to the unconscious woman.

"Yes." O'Connor pulled the mask back up.

"O'Connor," Richard said. "Bring her back safely."

O'Connor nodded and turned away.

Richard hated every single thing about this. He hated the pain and the prospect of having medsys remove the projectile from his arm. He hated that Eddie was in danger and might be hurt. He hated having to trust O'Connor. Most of all, he hated not being in control.

———

When we settle on a planet, it is imperative to pay attention to any indigenous plants and wildlife. It goes without saying that no Union species will consider establishing a settlement on any world where sentient life is already present, and as you might be aware, several survey teams conduct preliminary tests and examinations before a planet is cleared for anyone else to approach. But as important as it is to not accidentally or willfully disrupt a civilization, it is also of utmost importance not to ruin other life that may already be there.

If a planet has nothing that is considered life, complete planetforming is an option. This can take a long time, depending on how thoroughly conditions need to be altered for anyone to settle, and involve temporary biomes where scientists and other essential personnel live while slowly changing the planet. But in most cases, Union species will seek to settle on planets that already resemble their native worlds to some extent. Temperature, gravity, atmospheric composition, day cycle and weather conditions are some of the factors they will look at to begin with. After that, threat levels of the indigenous species will be thoroughly assessed.

Each Union member species has some autonomy, but everybody still has to go through the appropriate procedures and channels to ensure that a native animal is not wiped out just because they are venomous to the species that settles on the planet in question. If you are familiar with interstellar history, you will probably know what happened when the zetois found the planet called Zemahln today. This was a long time ago, even for the long-lived zetois, but everybody takes precautions to ensure nothing like that ever happens again.

Of course, everybody does not always see eye to eye about which creatures constitute significant life, and more often than not, åayu biologists are brought in to help, given their long history of cultivation and respect of any kind of animal and plant on every single world (including their native planet, which is nearly unique for a Union species!).

— Alannah Jackson, *Interstellar Sightseeing 101*

12

BIRD-WATCHING

Eddie did not like being left behind. Not because of abandonment issues, but because she wanted to be considered useful. And she was. She was perfectly good at sneaking into places, and picking locks, and avoiding surveillance. And running, and shooting a dart gun and whatever else was needed for this type of work. She also hated the fact that Richard had picked the guy who tried to murder him over her. But she had let it slide. Kierran O'Connor was not the better choice, but if there was one thing she liked even less than being left behind, it was the idea of leaving the enhanced soldier to keep watch. Because what would keep him from ditching them? Apart from the fact that Richard had yet to pay him, but it did not exactly strike Eddie as a radiation proof argument for him to stick around.

Eddie watched the two ex-soldiers move toward the house until they were obscured by the trees tastefully lining the perimeter of the estate. She stretched and decided to find a more comfortable position. No matter how professional and badass the two of them imagined they were, it would still take them a while to scale the building, disable alarms, get in, locate Spencer and slip back out with her.

Eddie glanced at her patch. She did have time for a game or two... But no. The whole idea of leaving her on watch duty was for her to keep, well, watch. Her last dose of hyper had almost worn off by now, and that meant she could not focus 100% on two or more things at the same time.

She wondered what Alannah was doing. Richard's job for her was straight-forward enough, even though it was a pretty strange one. One thing was for the mysterious Colonel to use Richard to get Spencer. That was what Richard meant to do all along, anyway. But using him as a messenger? That was weird. You'd think a TDF colonel would either send one of their own minions or else send a dispatch through VoidNet like everybody else. Trusting a random person to hand over a paper letter was weird.

A guard in a blue uniform appeared at the front door of the house. He didn't seem particularly alert. He was looking at his patch display and grinning at something on it. Then he spoke, but Eddie wasn't equipped with Richard's lip reading skills, so she had no idea what he was saying. Probably recording a message or talking to someone else on the local PlaNet. Well, that was good. The less alert security was, the easier it would be for Richard to do his job.

Something moved behind Eddie. For all she knew, it could be a squirrel or a similar local creature climbing up a tree. But she jumped to her feet and was spinning around, reaching for her dart gun before she had even registered what was going on.

"What are you doing here?" said one of the two people standing behind her.

Shit. Fuck. Damn. But her repertoire of curses would not get her off the hook. "Oh, hi," Eddie said, pretending to scratch her elbow instead of being about to unholster the gun inside her jacket. "You scared the hell out of me." She smiled and shook her head in mock self-deprecation. "I was bird-watching."

"Bird-watching?" echoed one of them. They were tall and had the stature of a draever. A small draever, at least. They were also wearing a discreet earpiece as well as a uniform identical to the one worn by the guard by the front door. The other person was wearing a matching uniform, and although he was a good bit less imposing, he was making up for that with the gun in his hand that looked suspiciously like a kinetic weapon.

"Yeah. Didn't you see the red-tailed diomedeid?" Eddie asked, hoping these people didn't know their spaceship classes. Or birds, for that matter.

"No," said the shorter of the two guards. "And neither did you, I bet."

"Well, only briefly," Eddie sighed. "I think you scared it away. But—"

"You are trespassing, young lady," he cut her off.

"Thank you," Eddie said. "It's been a while since anyone called me a lady. But is this private property? I followed the sound of the birds from the road."

The two guards exchanged a glance. "You'd better come with us," the bigger one said.

Eddie narrowed her eyes. "Where to?" she asked.

"We just want to talk," they replied, reaching out for Eddie's arm.

Eddie jerked away from them. "Nope!" she said. Richard had called her argumentative more than once. He meant it as an insult, but she never took it as such. "I'm pretty sure you can throw me off private property, but you can't take me in for interrogation against my will."

"Listen—" The guard broke off. They blinked, listening to something in the device in their ear.

"Shit," the shorter one said.

Eddie seconded that notion. Something had happened right now. Something that changed the situation. Eddie hoped it didn't have anything to do with Richard and Kierran, but she was not going to wait to find out. All three of them moved at the same time. Eddie brought up her dart gun and fired, hitting the short guard in the chest. The tall one lunged at her, and she barely managed to dodge.

———

115

"Drop your weapon!" the short guard shouted. He was not going down. Damn. He was wearing protection.

Eddie barreled into him, knocking both of them to the ground, the kinetic gun flying out of his hand and out of reach. She drew back for a punch, but the tall guard grabbed her from behind and pulled her back up.

She tried to send them flying, but they only ended up awkwardly draped over her back. This whole thing was going down the proverbial black hole really fast.

"Stop fighting!" they shouted.

And the short guard was getting back to his feet, going for his weapon.

That was it. She was not getting out of this one. But... Eddie kicked hard at the knee of the guard holding her. They yelped in pain, and for a moment, Eddie was free. She tore off her patch, threw it on the ground and stomped on it as hard and as many times as she could manage. It gave a crunching sound, and Eddie hoped it would be beyond repair.

And then the guards were on her again. The short one raised his gun, and for a horrifying moment, Eddie thought he would shoot her at point blank. But he turned the weapon and smashed the butt of it at her. She twisted, and the blow didn't land well, but her teeth snapped shut on her tongue, her jaw became a furnace of pain, and she did not see the next one coming. It hit her in the stomach, and she doubled over, heaving for breath.

One of the guards forced her arms back and clamped something around her wrists.

Eddie closed her eyes, gasping, coughing. Blood was pooling in her mouth.

"Bird-watching my ass," the guard behind her said with a scoff.

They dragged her back to the house. She didn't know if she ought to hope that Richard and Kierran had gotten away or that they hadn't. But it wouldn't matter one bit what she hoped, so she tried to pay attention to what was going on around her instead. Anything that might help her escape later.

The two guards manhandled Eddie into a tidy office with aesthetically pleasing, bland wall decorations and a vase that looked like Eddie could use it as a blunt weapon if given the chance.

"Sit," one of the guards said and roughly pushed her onto a chair. It would have felt more like the beginning of a serious interrogation if the chair was metal or even a simple plass stool. But this one was wonderfully soft with the sort of cushion that molded itself around your backside.

"I'm not a dog," Eddie snarled.

"I don't know, you seem like a bit of a bitch," one of the guards replied.

"And you seem like a first class asshole," Eddie retorted.

The other guard rolled their eyes as the first one began to reply, but then the door opened again, and this immediately made him shut up. The guards' boss, then?

The newcomer was short and meticulously dressed. She had a pinched look about her as if she was used to dealing with too much bullshit.

"Who's she?" the woman asked.

"We picked her up spying on the house, ma'am," a guard said.

"Really?" the woman said and, not waiting for an answer, turned to Eddie. "And what were you looking for?"

"Birds," Eddie repeated her story. "Look, I already told your friends here I'm sorry. I didn't notice I was trespassing. It was all because of that stupid bird."

"Why aren't you wearing a patch?" the woman asked, ignoring everything Eddie had said so far.

"I... dropped it," Eddie replied, frowning at her wrist as if she was only noticing it now.

"She threw it on the ground and jumped on it," the shorter guard said, helpfully. He handed the patch to the woman in charge. She inspected it with a frown on her face.

Eddie really hoped it was ruined. She probably could withstand some interrogation, but if her patch told them everything they wanted to know, the whole thing was screwed, Eddie included. Though she was pretty screwed already.

"She also had this," the tall guard said and produced Eddie's dart gun. She had been too preoccupied with being beaten up to notice exactly when they took it.

She wondered what Richard would do when he found her missing. Charge in to rescue her? Or... No, he wouldn't abandon her. That was not his style. And Alannah definitely wouldn't let him, anyway. If all else failed, Richard might trade her for Felicia Spencer, which would render the whole thing completely useless and a waste of time. There would be a rescue attempt. She was sure of that. So all she had to do was refuse to talk or send these people running in circles until that happened.

The woman sighed and handed Eddie's patch and dart gun back to the guards. "All right, then," she said. "Let's talk. What is your name?"

Eddie glared at her.

"This is your last chance," the woman continued. "What is your name?"

Last chance before what? Shockers and catchball bats and fingers bent over backwards until they snapped? Eddie swallowed. "Screw you," she said with more bravado than she felt.

"Fine. Have it your way. Keep an eye on her," the woman said, the last part to the two guards. She left the room in an efficient flurry of heels clicking on the stone floor.

"Can she do that without the boss's authorization?" one guard whispered to the other.

"It's not like she can ask her right now, is it?" the other replied.

Eddie stared straight ahead. Well, at least that meant Richard had been successful. She took a deep breath and half wished she had taken Alannah up on her offer to teach her some wendek breathing exercises.

As a human on Hestia, you are not going to look out of place. The people in the city of Oikos appear to be as diverse as anywhere else when it comes to their ethnic makeup and genders. If you are not human, however, you are likely to stand out. I asked my local guide how many percent of the city's population are made up of other species. He laughed and repeated the word in a way that suggested percentages do not even come in to play here. When pressed, he could think of just one åayu researcher who had been granted permission to stay for a few years. He also recalled encountering a wendek couple going sightseeing once. I haven't seen much of Oikos, but going through a largely pedestrian shopping area with my guide, I did not spot even one member of another species.

Most planets and stations will, apart from their predominant species, which is usually the one who built the space station or settled on the planet as the first, have a neighborhood made up of another species, have an interstellar tourist appeal, or at least have university professors, exchange students or immigrant families from other species.

Still, when I say you aren't going to look out of place as a human, you might still feel it if you are not fluent in the dominant lingua franca, which is Greek (despite the fact that less than 9% of the population are descendants of the Greek). If you do know modern Greek, you might still be thrown by the fact that the Olympians have what my guide calls "an antiquated understanding" of the language.

And that is just the language. Walking around the cityscape, it is easy to spot other differences. The current fashion here differs from most other human-dominated planets, and the social hierarchy is built not on democracy, but a kind of oligarchy.

— Alannah Jackson, *Hestia, Hubris & Hummus* (extremely temporary title!!)

13
CONTROL

"How may I help you today?" Medsys' inquiry was blinking for his attention on the display above the examination table.

"Just fix it," Richard groaned.

He had quickly sprayed wound sealant on his arm and given himself a shot of stimulants and painkillers in the chick in order to get back to the *Colibri*. His flying had still been less than graceful, and the sealant was a very temporary solution. But he had managed to get into the nest without destroying anything, had pulled Felicia Spencer out of the chick and deposited her in the cabin O'Connor had recently occupied, had locked the door and dragged himself to medbay. Getting onto the examination table had been such a relief that he wanted to close his eyes and relax for a few moments... But that would not do.

Medsys scanned his arm. Its diagnosis appeared, "You have a foreign object embedded in your area of complaint. I am going to anesthetize you, remove the object, decontaminate the wound and seal it. Please be aware that you will have to keep the area of complaint immobilized for—"

"Local anesthetics only," Richard said, not bothering to read the rest. He would rather have ignored the injury for now, but that was a very bad idea for a lot of very good reasons.

"Understood." Medsys jabbed a syringe into his arm in two different locations.

As numbness began to spread all the way from his shoulder to his forearm, Richard allowed himself to close his eyes anyway. It wasn't that he would get queasy from looking at the procedure. He'd seen wound sealant being pulled off and bullets removed before, a couple of times from his own body. But he needed to think. He needed to plan. And this was as good a time as any.

Felicia Spencer was probably coming to at this point, so he would need to talk to her. Not that he owed her anything, but he might be able to extract useful information from her. Or be able to use her as leverage if O'Connor did not succeed in retrieving Eddie... Richard sighed. Eddie. He should be the one to rescue her. Not O'Connor. He felt the urge to try to reach her patch, but given the circumstances, that would be stupid.

Medsys' equipment made a nauseating, wet sucking sort of noise followed by a clonk when it dropped the projectile into a container.

Richard would have to contact Alannah soon. She must be starting to wonder what was taking them so long. Though, perhaps he should wait until Eddie was back in order not to worry her unnecessarily... Then again, he would rather not leave Spencer alone on the *Colibri*, and he would have to go back to the planet for O'Connor and Eddie. In fact, the sooner he could go, the better.

Richard opened his eyes again. Medsys was disinfecting the bullet wound now. As he watched, its spindly, mechanical arm finished the job and began to reapply wound sealant. He raised his uninjured arm and found Alannah's contact info on his patch.

Her face appeared on the display a moment later. "Yes?" she said.

"Did you take care of the task I gave you?" Richard asked.

"Yes," Alannah said again. "Are you lying down? Are you in medbay? Are you injured?"

"Yes to all of that," Richard admitted, "but it's nothing serious."

Alannah's eyebrows drew down. "And the others? Did you do... the thing?"

"We did," Richard told her. "However, complications arose. Eddie went missing, but O'Connor is retrieving her."

"Missing? How?" Alannah asked, her eyes growing wide and alarmed now.

"We think she was taken by people working for our target. I trust that O'Connor will get her back. But even if he should fail, they will have figured out Eddie is connected to the disappearance of their boss, so they won't harm her." A bit of a stretch. They wouldn't kill her, at least.

"They abducted Eddie?" Alannah exclaimed, then glanced around furtively.

"Yes. And I would appreciate it if you could refrain from telling the whole city," Richard said.

Judging from Alannah's expression, his attempt at being flippant fell flat. "Have you tried calling her?" she asked.

"No. That would only alert her abductors to a lot of things I don't want them to know."

Alannah's lips compressed in dismay for a moment. "I should go help Kierran," she said.

"No!" Richard told her. "Absolutely not. I don't want to endanger you as well. I need you to get back to the ship as soon as—"

Alannah shook her head. "I need to talk to someone," she said.

"Talk to someone? Alannah, this is not up for debate!"

But he was already on hold. Alannah had put him on hold! Richard growled and punched the side of the examination table.

"Your heart rate and blood pressure have become elevated," medsys informed him, unhelpfully. "Are you experiencing discomfort or anxiety?"

"I'm experiencing lack of control of a tourist guide writer!" Richard snarled.

"I'm sorry. I cannot recognize your complaint. Please select the option which matches your experience best from the list on the display," medsys suggested.

"Never mind. Are you done? Can I leave?"

"The procedure is done. However, you are advised to stay in medbay for a minimum of two hours for monitoring of your vital signs."

Richard sat up and ignored medsys. The projectile wound had been neatly sealed. But medsys kept giving him advice that bordered on polite orders. He took a rudimentary sling out from a cupboard since it seemed faster than waiting for medsys to get around to it.

His patch spoke. Or rather, Alannah had finally taken him off hold again and was talking. "What?" he snapped. "Alannah, you need to—"

She made a placating gesture. "Richard, please listen to me. Or—" She cut herself off and winced apologetically. "Or, you know. I delivered the letter as you asked, and the recipient is with me now. He's... Julien?"

The camera moved. A fresh-faced, bright-eyed youth appeared on the display. "Richard Hart, sir," he said, "I'm Lieutenant Julien Teresi."

"Of course you are," Richard muttered under his breath, hoping the kid wasn't as good at lipreading as he was. Somehow, he was not surprised to learn that the person who was supposedly Micah Dietrich's deep cover agent in Oikos was a charming and handsome person. It probably wasn't a job requirement, but having a face that made people like you was often a good quality for someone in that position.

"Yes, sir," the Lieutenant continued, apparently quite good at lipreading, anyway, and not missing a beat, "I was advised to aid you in any way you need."

"Were you, now," Richard sighed.

"Or the person who delivered the letter. But since Alannah works for you, I imagine that is what the Colonel meant."

Richard was also not particularly surprised to learn this. Dietrich had not overtly gotten involved in the mess, but they had still enlisted an agent. Despite Richard telling them he did not need the help, and without telling him about it. Damn their secrecy. But then, what was an intelligence officer if not secretive? It was practically in their job description. Richard of all people knew that. Still...

"And how exactly is it that you plan on assisting me?" he asked.

"Alannah says you have two agents missing," the Lieutenant said. "May I offer to retrieve them? You are probably aware that I can't officially step in as an officer, but I imagine they will at least need transport from their location to your ship."

Richard took a deep breath. As much as he would prefer not to involve the agent and end up in what Dietrich would probably consider their debt, he could see the sense in this. Except... O'Connor. "And you will report back to Colonel Dietrich?" Richard asked.

The Lieutenant's brow creased. "Yes, sir. Is that a problem?"

Yes. Yes, it was. But the stimulants were wearing off, and Richard knew he wasn't operating at full capacity. If it came to a fight, he would be inefficient. Even flying a chick was difficult and potentially dangerous with one arm in a sling. His own risk assessment told him that Eddie would be safer with the eager Lieutenant than with him, and her safety was the most important factor. Besides, O'Connor wasn't stupid. He wasn't going to shake the agent's hand with his artificial one and introduce himself as the guy who failed at killing Richard Hart.

"Sir?"

"Yes," Richard said. "Your help would be greatly appreciated."

The kid actually gave him a happy grin. "Where do you need me to go?"

"Alannah can tell you," Richard said, trusting that Dietrich's agent would know where the Spencer residence was located or at least be able to quickly find out. "Your priority is to keep my people safe and make sure they get back to my ship. Understood?"

Teresi's expression turned serious. "Yes, sir." And then he saluted. Of course he saluted.

"Good. Give me Alannah for a moment," Richard said, deciding that explaining he wasn't an officer anymore was irrelevant right now.

The camera moved back to Alannah.

"Stay safe," Richard told her. "That is not a suggestion. It's an order. I don't want you to complicate things."

"I'm not—"

"Woolly cuties," Richard said flatly, which no doubt sounded like code to someone like Teresi, although it was a very straight-forward reminder of her antics rushing headlong into a dangerous situation the first time they met.

"Gotcha," Alannah said with a smile that looked a bit embarrassed.

The conversation had taken Richard all the way from medbay to the cabin where the woman who wanted him dead was locked up. He stopped. Closed his eyes and tried to roll his shoulders to loosen up tense muscles, but one of them being connected to his arm, this was not a great idea. He hated injuries. He hated relying on others. But there really wasn't much to do about it at this point. He straightened his spine and unlocked the door.

Felicia Spencer was awake and in the middle of pacing back and forth in the small space. She started when the door slid open, but quickly hid it behind a glare.

"Hello," Richard said.

"You," Spencer said in the way you'd usually say "jerk" or "asshole".

This time, Richard replied instead of shooting her. "Yes. Me."

"What happened to your arm?" she asked. "Is it serious?"

"Afraid not. I'm not going to keel over dead anytime soon," Richard said. "Turns out I'm not very easy to kill."

"You kidnapped me. Don't think you'll get away with this!" she spat.

"You had an assassin attempt to kill me. You hardly have any moral high ground here."

"You can't prove anything." She crossed her arms over her chest.

"As a matter of fact, I can." Richard smiled. "You went through an agent who goes by the name Egis. He told us everything."

Her face screwed up. "You ruined my marriage! You ruined my whole life!"

Richard blinked. Then turned around, looking at the corners where the walls met the ceiling before glancing back at his prisoner. "Where's the camera and why wasn't I told I'm starring in a bad drama?"

"You are not even taking this seriously," she scoffed.

"Oh, I assure you I am. I am taking it very seriously that you thought being caught cheating warranted having me killed. And so is the Terran Defense Force, as it happens."

"I am just trying to live a peaceful life on Hestia!" she said, as if Richard had somehow endangered that with his mere existence. "What about my child?"

"She lives with her father," Richard reminded her.

Felicia Spencer shook her head. "Well, she is in my house right now. Do you even realize how traumatizing all this will be to her? Her mother being brutally kidnapped."

Richard kept his face neutral. But damn. That was poor timing. "She will be informed that you are well as soon as possible," he said. "Now, I have a few questions."

"What makes you think I have any answers?"

"The fact that I may let you record a message for your daughter and make sure she gets it before we leave Olympian space?" Richard suggested. He didn't like using a child to bribe her, but the kid wouldn't know.

"You are a horrible man, Richard Hart," Spencer said.

"I'll take that as a compliment," he replied.

Witnesses saw Terran Defense Force officers escort three residents of the Amesbury quarter away yesterday around noon. While there has been no official announcements from the military or even civilian law enforcement on Stonehenge, another such arrest took place later the same day.

It has also been noted that three of the Terran Defense Force's Strigiformes class ships usually stationed at Stonehenge have been dispatched in a hurry. While this could be related to routine tasks, the timing is remarkable.

Colonel Micah Dietrich, head of military security, has not been available for questions, but we did encounter a Lieutenant Nakano who works directly under them. According to him, "There is absolutely nothing to be worried about. The Terran Defense Force is just doing its work."

— Alice Merriweather, Stonehenge News

14
RETRIEVAL

As he turned away from his accidental contractor's retreating form, it did occur to Kierran O'Connor that he could disappear without a trace right now. He could simply walk away from this place, find a ship bound for a destination far away from Hestia, far away from Stonehenge and Hawking, Dwebl, or anywhere else that someone might think of looking for him. It would be easy. Kierran owed these people nothing. He had made a deal with Richard Hart out of necessity and nothing else. Eddie had not given him any reason to do her any favors. It was all strictly about business. And about not being handed over to the Terran Defense Force.

A very irrelevant thought briefly introduced itself. Kierran dismissed it. He had no obligations to Alannah, either. Yes, she had been kind to him for no apparent reason, but that was her own weakness to deal with. Not his.

Still... He had never run away from a contract before with the exception of the hit on Richard Hart, which he had not run away from. That was not the term for what had happened.

He bent down to examine the ground. There had definitely been a scuffle here. The grass looked trampled, and he could detect footprints by Eddie and two other people, unless he was mistaken, which he usually wasn't.

He picked up a small bit of plass. A piece of a screen? Possibly a patch. Durable though they were, it was possible to crack the screen if enough force was applied. That suggested someone had purposefully tried to destroy it or, he supposed, the wrist to which it was attached.

He wouldn't get anything out of lingering here. The faster he went about the task of retrieving the sourly pilot, the better. He set off toward the house again. There was really no point in trying to sneak in this time. The abduction had been discovered already, and Felicia Spencer's people would have found their last point of entry and posted extra security everywhere.

Kierran unholstered the dart gun Richard Hart had equipped him with. An inadequate weapon in itself with its harmless projectiles, but it would do for now.

In a way, he thought as he approached the front entrance of the building, it was a relief not to have to work with other people. Richard Hart wasn't bad, but he was slower than Kierran and could easily become a liability. It was so much easier to do this on his own.

The two guards stationed at the door raised their weapons and shouted at Kierran to stop and identify himself. Instead of replying or slowing down, he closed his organic eye and honed in on their exposed throats. Two darts. That was all he needed. The guards fired back before collapsing, but dodging the shots was easy.

Kierran picked one of the unconscious guards up by the collar of her uniform, held her in front of the retina scanner next to the front door and pried open her eyelid. He dropped her on the ground again and confiscated the guns from both, disabling one and tossing it aside and stuffing the other one into his holster.

Time to locate Eddie. It was anyone's guess where they would have taken her, but Kierran could narrow it down easily enough. His inorganic eye identified four heat signatures within the building. One was not human-shaped. A pet, probably. He wondered what kind of pet— And shook that thought right out of his head. Only Alannah would care about something as irrelevant as that. He would start on the ground level and work his way up.

As soon as he kicked in the door to the first room containing heat sources, Kierran knew this wasn't the right one. There were two people in here, and none of them was Eddie. He brought up the dart gun and shot one of them as the unarmed man was turning around with an expression of surprise on his face.

The second person in the room was a child, and Kierran surprised himself by hesitating. The darts weren't lethal. They would do no lasting damage to adults, and this child was grown enough that the same would be the case for her.

"You took my mother!" she screamed and launched herself at Kierran, oblivious to the fact that he was armed and much bigger than her.

He had never fought a child before. He caught her wrists and closed his artificial hand around them.

"Let go! You're hurting me! Give me back my mother!" she screamed.

Kierran had to shut her up before she alerted the whole household to his presence. "Quiet!" he said. "Or I will break your wrists."

The child shut up. She was biting her lip, though, and her eyes were welling up with tears.

This was needlessly complicated. Richard Hart had said Spencer had a child, but also that the kid lived with her father. Well, whether she was visiting or if the intel was incorrect did not matter. Kierran had a child at gunpoint. She could be used as leverage. He could insist on trading her for Eddie. But... No. Too much trouble.

The child was staring up at him. He needed to just shoot her or tie her up and gag her. The former was a lot more time-efficient—

And then he heard voices and footsteps outside the room. So the child's screams had alerted someone, after all.

Kierran swung around with the girl still held by her wrists. She shrieked in terror. As the two uniformed guards entered, Kierran rapidly fired a dart at each of them because he couldn't reach for the kinetic gun without letting go of the child. The problem with darts, of course, was that they did take a few seconds to work. One of the newcomers managed to bring up their own gun and fire even as their knees were buckling under them. But their aim was completely off.

Kierran let go of the child and intercepted the projectile with his own arm. There was no logical reason for that. The dart glanced harmlessly off the metal, only tearing at the fabric of his sleeve before it practically bounced. The child shrieked again. There was a bloody streak on her cheek now. She was reaching up to touch her face when her eyes went unfocused. She slumped against Kierran, and he lowered her to the floor. Well, that was one problem solved. He wouldn't need to shoot her, after all. That was... strangely relieving.

He picked up the dart. It was marked with a B. Not lethal, but a shade more serious than what Richard had issued him with. That explained why such a superficial hit would impact the child so thoroughly.

Kierran picked up the dart gun on his way out of the room and disabled it. The other guard's gun was kinetic. Kierran disabled that one too.

His next room of choice proved to be the right one. Three people were located inside. A handcuffed person in a chair, Eddie, another uniformed guard, and a woman standing close to Eddie. The guard never managed to reach for his weapon before Kierran removed him from the board. The woman was starting to protest when Kierran shot her. He ignored them both and approached Eddie.

"Kierran!" she said, grinning up at him. Which was... Strange. Was she in shock?

"Are you hurt?" he asked, searching her with his gaze, but apart from a few bruises on her face and dried blood on her lips, she appeared intact. Her heart rate was perfectly calm too. Almost too calm.

Eddie's expression darkened. "I was hurt when my sister decided not to talk to me anymore because of my addiction and didn't want me to see my nephew because I might be a bad influence on him," she told him.

Kierran blinked. Was there a kind of brain injury that caused people to relive their past and completely ignore the present situation? Or could this be attributed to shock? Not important. He wasn't being paid nearly enough to speculate. "Hold still," he said and bent over her.

"That," Eddie said, "is not something I'm very good at."

"How about shutting up?" he asked.

"Hah!" Eddie babbled. "You aren't as uptight and stoic as you pretend to be."

Kierran did not deign to reply. Instead, he curled the fingers of his prosthetic hand around the chain of her handcuffs and yanked.

"Ow!" Eddie exclaimed when the chain snapped.

Kierran pulled her to her feet. She swayed.

They must have drugged her. And Kierran thought he recognized the signs, but... "Can you walk?" he asked.

"Yes," Eddie confirmed, staggering a couple of steps sideways before steadying herself.

Maybe she could. But she wouldn't be able to run, and she wouldn't be able to follow any orders. She would be too much of a liability. There was really only one logical way to get her out of this place.

Kierran hoisted her up and more or less tossed her over his shoulder.

"Oi! Hey!" Eddie cried. "Haven't I been kidnapped enough for one day?"

"Be quiet and hold still," Kierran told her, "or I will dart you."

"You absolute freak," Eddie replied, but in a barely audible mutter, which was fine. That wouldn't distract him.

Kierran jogged out of the room with Eddie bouncing on his shoulder, only pausing to pick up the sad remnants of her patch that had been left on a table.

On occasion, the Terran Defense Force finds a detainee unwilling to cooperate during questioning. If the matter pertains to serious crime, and the circumstantial evidence is convincing, the Terran Defense Force might find it necessary to conduct a pharmaceutically assisted interrogation. This is far more lenient on the subject than earlier methods of interrogation. (For further reading on military interrogation techniques through history: See *History*.)

The drug in question is called aletheia. It is a mild tranquilizer with a discreet hallucinogenic effect that makes the subject pliable. In short, it makes the detainee comfortable, talkative, and liable to association.

Despite aletheia not being a truth drug in the strictest sense of the word, it makes the subject want to say whatever occurs to them. In an interrogation situation, the topic of said matter will naturally be on their mind.

However, although everything the subject divulges is the truth as they know it, it takes a skilled and authorized interrogator to be able to ask the questions that will reveal the right answers to aid the investigation. And given the delicate nature of pharmaceutically assisted interrogations, it also takes expertise to keep the subject's associations from straying into unpleasant territory. In order to ensure both the usefulness of the interrogation as well as the wellbeing of the subject, only those who have completed the appropriate courses and are certified aletheia interrogators are allowed to conduct this kind of questioning. (For further reading: See *Specialization; Intelligence*.)

The effect of aletheia will naturally dissipate entirely within a few hours. However, it is recommended to keep the subject under surveillance for at least an hour after the interrogation. To reduce any discomfort the subject may experience, it is also advised to supply them with anti-nausea and potentially pain-relieving medication as they may experience symptoms similar to post-alcohol intoxication.

On rare occasions, the subject may need counseling after an aletheia-assisted interrogation. This is not because of the substance itself, but due to any unwanted associations that may have surfaced during the questioning.

For further reading on interrogation related to internal affairs: See *Failsafe*.

— Excerpt from internal Terran Defense Force document

15
THE TRUTH AND OTHER IRRELEVANT THINGS

Julien was a conscientious driver. He navigated through Oikos with ease and consideration for other people in the streets. The car's speakers were pouring out a song in English about losing your significant other because apparently they had not been so significant as to keep you from cheating on them. About how sad it was and how you wanted to do anything to get them back.

Alannah tried not to look shifty. It was just a song. Not Julien's comment on this whole thing. He didn't even know what the job was about. He claimed that he only had instructions to assist. Alannah hoped her nebulous explanations would keep him from asking too many questions. She had tried to keep her lies to a minimum, and he had accepted her statement that she didn't know very much about the whole thing because she was just a civilian working for Richard.

"Your boss seemed reluctant to let me help," he commented blithely as he swerved around another car.

"Richard is very independent," Alannah replied. Not only that. He didn't want the military to know about Kierran. That he had agreed to this at all was a small miracle. Or a testament of how much he cared about Eddie.

Julien nodded and turned down a less busy road.

"So, do you do this a lot?" she prompted.

"No," Julien said airily. "Usually my commanding officer calls the shots, but this is such a simple thing that it wasn't necessary to run it by her. Or *was* such a simple thing," he added, "until it turned out to be about abducting and saving people."

"I'm... sorry?" Alannah said.

"Oh, don't be!" Julien flashed her a quick grin. "Without disclosing too much, I can tell you being under cover on Hestia isn't particularly exciting most of the time. I have gotten really good at making black brew foam, though."

"I could tell," Alannah laughed.

"Thank you," Julien said. "We get some pretty arbitrary life skills as agents. Just take Dietrich. Rumor has it they were a waiter at one point. And a model too."

"I see." Alannah's mental image of Richard's mysterious Colonel changed from that of a stern, bulky soldier to someone more akin to Julien himself.

"Let's take this road out of the city," Julien continued. He turned down a smaller street that led them out of the densely populated area to the open country.

Minutes later, the car pulled up by the curb some hundred meters from the property of Felicia Spencer.

The seat belts retracted, and Julien checked the rear view camera. "Maybe you should stay here," he said.

"That is going to be a no from me," Alannah replied. "For so many reasons."

He shot her a sidelong glance. "All right. I didn't think you would, but it's the sort of thing I have to say to civilians." He reached under the seat. "Here," he said as he handed something to her.

"Is that a bulletproof vest?" Alannah asked, taking the surprisingly heavy piece of clothing. It looked too flimsy to be efficient.

"Shock repelling vest," Julien said. "Which is kind of the same thing, but it's an all-rounder for different kinds of weapon types. And not as efficient as military grade armor, but... Anyway, you can wear it under your clothes. I am." He pulled up his shirt to show her the snug-fitting vest.

"Right," Alannah said. As she began to take off the outer layer of clothes, Julien excavated several objects from the recesses of his car. Alannah felt mildly indignant and disconcerted to discover that the Lieutenant had a whole arsenal of weapons sitting under the seats and in compartments under the dashboard. "I'm just asking out of curiosity," she said, "but do you expect to need all that... equipment? Ki— um, Richard's other associate is supposed to find Eddie and get her out."

"Who exactly is that associate, again?" Julien asked, his voice intensely casual.

"I haven't talked very much to him, but Richard says he's really good at things like this," felt like a lie although it was all perfectly true.

"Well, that doesn't mean I should go unarmed," Julien said and stuffed a very small gun into one of his boots. "Do you need a weapon, or are you good? Only, if I lend you one, we have to fill out some forms afterward and pretend we did it before I gave it to you."

"It's fine," Alannah said. No, she was not armed with anything but her wits and a dictation tool on her patch, but they weren't supposed to get into trouble. Just pick up Eddie and Kierran and get them to the *Colibri*. Which she was really, really anxious to do. "Can we go now?"

Julien nodded. He pulled a courtesy mask over his face. "Okay, let's go," he said, slightly muffled as the fabric covered his mouth and nose.

They started towards the looming building in the middle of a huge lawn that Alannah could not help but think of as exposed. But she had to trust that Kierran had gotten rid of any threats.

Two guards were slumped on the ground next to the entrance. Unconscious or dead?

Julien, one of his guns held in front of him in both hands, approached them. He prodded one with his foot, then the other. "They were darted," he reported in a hushed sort of voice.

Alannah nodded. If Kierran had killed any of them, she would have been extremely disappointed in him. She found that she was relieved and a tiny bit proud that he hadn't.

Julien pushed open the unlocked door with his elbow and went in, gun at the ready once again. It was a fancy home with a luxurious entrance hall adorned with pieces of art that Alannah would very much have liked to study under different circumstances.

"Maybe we should wait here," she suggested in a whisper. But then there was a noise from somewhere in the building. A clatter followed by an exclamation of something that might be either fear or pain. And Alannah recognized the voice. "Eddie!" she gasped and, despite her previous resolve, she started forward.

"Hey!" Julien stage-whispered at her and overtook her in a few long strides. "Stay behind me!"

"Sorry," Alannah replied. "But Eddie—"

Julien shook his head and then turned his attention on the corridor ahead. The place was eerily quiet and empty but for the sound of Alannah's breathing and hammering heart. And then footsteps from up ahead as they approached a corner. Julien shot one look back at her over his shoulder, held up a finger that probably meant she should stay put and be quiet, and then flung himself around the corner, gun at the ready. "Don't move, and don't make a sound!" he said in a lower, more menacing voice than Alannah had thought him capable of.

"Drop your—" another voice began. A familiar voice.

"Stop!" Alannah cried and jumped out from behind Julien. "Don't shoot!" And then, "Eddie!"

Kierran was standing in front of them with a gun pointed at Julien. But more importantly, he had someone in very tight ecoleather pants flung like a bag of ripeths over his shoulder.

"Alannah?" came the wobbly voice of the pilot.

"Put her down now!" Julien demanded.

"No," Kierran simply said.

And the stupid, stubborn soldier boys were still pointing their respective guns at each other. It was the worst, most irrelevant standoff Alannah had ever seen. Admittedly, she had only seen the ones on shows like *Worra & Darith*, but this was decidedly more superfluous than any of those, and that was saying something.

"Stop!" Alannah repeated, trying to sound authoritative and still not speak too loudly.

"He has your pilot!" Julien said.

"Yes, thankfully!"

"He is threatening me," Kierran said, staring intently at Julien.

This would be deeply amusing if not for the fact that Alannah still didn't know if Eddie was okay, and if weapons weren't involved. "We are all on the same side!" Alannah gestured at Kierran. "This is the associate Richard sent to retrieve Eddie. And this," she pointed at Julien, "is... another associate who is helping us."

"Then he should stand down," Kierran said.

Julien shifted, but he didn't lower his weapon.

"Oh for the love of—" Alannah groaned. "Eddie, can you kick him?"

"Yes," Eddie replied with a weird, little giggle. "May I? I really want to."

"No," Alannah sighed, although she could not help smiling in relief. "You will both put away your stupid guns on three, or I will slap you, Julien, and Eddie will kick you, Kierran." Probably not a very effective threat to two soldiers, but at least it showed she meant it. "One. Two. Three!"

Miraculously, both boys lowered their firearms.

"Thank you!" Alannah said. "Now, let's get out of here." And since she was already issuing orders and the two of them seemed to take them, she continued, "Julien, you go first. Kierran, follow him. I bring up the rear." Mostly because she wanted to see Eddie's face.

"Hi," Eddie said, grinning at her from her upside-down position.

"Are you hurt? Why is he carrying you?" Alannah asked.

"I'm fine," Eddie reassured her although her face was bruised, and her eyes didn't look entirely focused.

"Talk later," Kierran suggested.

Alannah really wanted to hear what the hell had happened to Eddie and also hug her tightly, but she decided that he was right.

They made it back to Julien's car with no complications. Kierran deposited Eddie on the backseat where she slumped down and slid sideways.

Alannah insisted on getting in next to her, which left Kierran to take the front seat next to Julien. She did consider the wisdom of it, but she trusted they wouldn't try to kill each other while Julien was driving them to safety.

Kierran and Julien both pulled off their masks. Julien tossed his over his shoulder to the backseat. Kierran stuffed his into a pocket.

"What happened?" Alannah asked Eddie who opted for laying down with her head in Alannah's lap as the car swung away from the curb at a speed that probably wasn't entirely in compliance with local traffic laws.

"They interrogated me," Eddie said.

"Did they torture you?"

"No, no. It was fun," Eddie reassured her.

Alannah was no expert on interrogation techniques, but she was fairly certain the procedure ought not to be fun for the person being interrogated.

"You want—" Julien began.

"She must—" Kierran said at the same time.

Alannah looked up to see them both staring straight ahead, their necks and shoulders tense. "What?" Alannah demanded.

"Who is that guy?" Eddie asked. "He isn't your boyfriend or anything, is he?"

"No," Alannah told her and patted her hair.

"Good," Eddie said earnestly.

"After you," Julien told Kierran, a little too sweetly.

"She must have been drugged with aletheia or something similar," Kierran said.

"*Something similar* doesn't exist," Julien said, his voice getting dangerously close to a perfect imitation of Kierran's tone and accent.

"I didn't do anything!" Eddie whined. "I only take the doses of hyper that I need for jumping. I swear!"

"I know," Alannah said, soothingly.

"I'm sure it's aletheia," Julien continued. "Which is why you want to take blood samples as soon as you can so you have proof."

"What exactly is aletheia?" Alannah asked.

"It's a drug used by the military to assist with interrogations," Julien said. "Civilians should not have it."

"A truth drug?" Alannah asked.

"No, I only told them what I wanted to," Eddie said. "You smell nice, Alannah."

"Thank you," Alannah said, smiling reassuringly down at Eddie and trying not to get distracted.

"She's right, actually," Julien continued. "That's how aletheia works. It relaxes you and makes you talk. She only told them what she wanted, but the drug might have made her want to tell them confidential things. Your boss needs to debrief her."

"Why have I never heard of this drug before?" Alannah asked.

"It's not something the Force makes a habit of talking about. You also have to be a really good interrogator to control the subjects because their associations tend to run wild," Julien explained.

"Yes," Kierran confirmed.

Alannah caught Julien briefly eying him. "Speaking from personal experience?" he asked.

"I have never conducted an aletheia interrogation," Kierran said which, Alannah was pretty sure, was not at all what Julien had asked.

"How long until it wears off?" Alannah asked.

Eddie was snuggling up to her, which Alannah did not mind at all. But she did mind that Eddie didn't have much control over what she did and said. Honesty was a cornerstone of any relationship, but it shouldn't come out of intoxication of any kind.

"A few hours," Julien said. "She'll probably have a bit of a hangover after that."

"I always drink responsibly!" Eddie chimed in. "And I go by the rules with hyper, too. I promise."

"I know," Alannah told her. "No one is blaming you for anything." She shifted a bit to be able to pull up a display on her patch. "I'll inform Richard that we are on the way."

"Sure," Julien agreed.

"Where are you taking us?" Kierran asked.

Julien snorted. "Back to your ship, of course."

"Via commercial chick?" Kierran asked.

"No. We have a private chick for occasions like this. It's faster and easier. And safer. By now, it's probably widely known that Spencer is missing."

"And security will let us go?" Alannah asked.

"Yes," Julien said.

"Why?" Kierran asked.

"Because I say so," Julien told him. "Come on, have some faith in me. I'm helping you out, aren't I?"

"That's really nice of you," Eddie piped up. "You're okay, Julius. I like you better than Kierran. I would rather eat a hot dog with you. But I would much, much rather eat one with Alannah."

There was an awkward moment of silence.

"So you are a Terran Defense Force agent?" Kierran surmised.

Julien drummed at the steering wheel with his fingers, considering. "Alannah and your boss already know, and I guess anyone with two braincells could figure that out anyway," he sighed.

"Wow, you don't look like a soldier at all," Eddie exclaimed.

"That's kind of the point," Julien said.

"Richard does," Eddie continued. "And Kierran—"

Alannah slapped her hand across Eddie's mouth. "Sweetie, Julien has to focus on driving. He doesn't need to know what Kierran thinks of Richard." She smiled apologetically down at Eddie's confused face. That had not been what the pilot was about to say at all, of course. But Alannah fervently hoped Julien wouldn't ask any questions none of them wanted to answer. Well, none of them except Eddie. "You know," she added for distraction, "I just need to do a quick change. I borrowed Julien's shock proof vest for this." The only one distracted by that was Eddie who gazed up at her in a way that Alannah decided not to interpret, given the circumstances.

News report disturbance at prytaneis member Spencer's home. I am still detained at meeting with F. Look into it discreetly.
—C

I am going to need your report on Spencer asap.
—C

Julien?
—C

Julien Teresi, get your head out of your latte art and report!
—C

Julien NOW!!
—C

Sorry, I was busy!
—J

Don't worry about the Spencer thing btw.
—J

REPORT!!!
—C

— Written correspondence between Captain Cora Moretti and Lieutenant Julien Teresi

16
INTERSTELLAR MILITARY PENPALS

Despite a reassuring message from Alannah, Richard could not stop pacing until the *Colibri* alerted him that her chick bay was opening up the outer airlock. He waited for the nondescript-looking chick to settle in next to the ship's own chick, waited for the outer doors to close again, and for the panel in front of him to finally turn green before he was able to enter the chick bay.

After the quick decontamination procedure, O'Connor was first out. He gave Richard a brief nod. Richard resisted the urge to immediately demand the dart gun back, and also the additional weapons which O'Connor seemed to have picked up. Because now Lieutenant Teresi appeared too.

"Captain Hart, sir!" he said and saluted crisply.

"Captain of a ship, not captain in the Force," Richard told him, refusing to return the salute. "Thank you for bringing back my people."

"Oh. My pleasure," Teresi said, morphing into a less soldierly version of himself immediately.

Richard needed to talk more to him, but right now he had to check on Eddie. Alannah was leading her out of the chick, holding on to her elbow as if she had trouble walking. And Richard had no idea what to make of his pilot's expression. Was that embarrassment? Or worry?

"Good job, Alannah," Richard said. "Eddie—"

"Shit, are you okay?" Eddie interrupted. She was staring at his arm with an eerily concerned look on her face.

"I'm fine," Richard replied. "And you?" He was beginning to worry that she might be in shock after what had happened. An interrogation could mean a lot of things. She didn't look too roughed up, but...

"Yeah," Eddie said. "Fuck, Richard, is that my fault for getting caught?"

"Fault has nothing to do with it," he replied. "What did they do to you? Do you need to go to medbay?"

"Nah, I'm good." Eddie smiled. "All ready to fly!"

"No!" Alannah said before Richard did.

One of the others, Teresi, Richard thought, said something.

"Yes," Alannah said. "They used something called aletheia to interrogate her. Julien says we should get a blood sample so we have evidence."

"Aletheia? How the hell did they—" Richard cut himself off. It certainly explained Eddie's changed personality. "No, how long ago was this?"

Teresi said something again. A long something. Nobody seemed to have told him about Richard's disability.

"It should wear off soon," Alannah summed up the Lieutenant's monologue.

"Thank you," Richard said. "And good."

Eddie ran a hand across her face. "Oh shit," she muttered.

"Eddie?"

"Just... starting to realize I might have said a lot of... stuff."

"About us? About taking Spencer? About the Force?" Richard asked.

"No," Eddie groaned. "About Alannah's hair and a lot of other things."

"It's okay. I'm glad you like my hair," Alannah said and patted her arm.

"But the interrogation, Eddie!" Richard prompted her.

"Don't worry. I don't know what that truth drug is supposed to be like, but I just kind of associated to a bunch of subjects that didn't have much to do with their questions. And then Kierran came."

This time Richard turned when Teresi started talking again.

"—as far as I know. So the drug did work, but if there was still any hyper left in her body, that might account for her ability to go off on a tangent. Plus, they probably weren't trained properly for a pharmaceutically assisted interrogation. I'm not even cleared to do that," he finished.

Richard was. And he knew exactly how tricky they could be. "Okay," he said. "Alannah, will you take her to medbay and get that blood sample? And get her some fluids and painkillers for the hangover. You will feel like you have one when the drug wears off," he added to Eddie. Dammit. The good thing was that there was no physical complications when mixing hyper with aletheia, but it would still be a rough ride for her because they needed to get away from Rheia as quickly as possible.

"Thank you for your help, Julien," Alannah told Teresi, leaving Eddie's side for a brief moment to hug him before she began to herd Eddie out.

"If you don't have anything to add, maybe you should go with them?" Richard suggested to O'Connor. "We will talk later." Meaning he was going to take his dart gun back and also the other weapons. And pay O'Connor too, of course.

O'Connor nodded and turned on his heel to follow the others. He probably wanted to be in vicinity of a Terran Defense Force officer as much as Richard wanted him to be, which was not at all.

"Thank you again. Is there anything I should know from your perspective?" Richard asked Teresi.

The young Lieutenant shrugged. "Not really. I just followed orders."

"May I ask," Richard began, "what exactly that letter from Colonel Dietrich said?"

"Sure. They asked the recipient of the letter to assist in any way you needed it," Teresi said. "So that's what I did."

Richard had figured it was something like that. That was the whole reason he had asked Alannah to hand it over so whatever agent was on Hestia did not get involved in his business. Not that it had worked. "I can't help noticing you aren't called Cora," he said.

Teresi flashed him a grin. "No, I'm not. She wasn't available, and I assessed the situation and decided it was better for me to assist than wait for her."

"I see," Richard said. Appearances could deceive, especially when it came to deep cover agents, but even so, it might be a good thing that Teresi's superior officer hadn't gotten involved in all this.

"I should get back to Oikos," Teresi said. "But would you mind giving this to Colonel Dietrich?" He retrieved an envelope from a pocket. It was a bit crumbled after sitting in his pants.

"Of course," Richard said, meaning that yes, of course he would mind. He took the envelope.

"If they ask, I wrote it in a hurry. My handwriting isn't... Well, I'm not the Colonel." He smiled sheepishly. "So that friend of yours, Kierran..."

"Yes?" Richard said, trying not to look like his insides were twisting into a knot.

"He's pretty cool, huh?"

Richard made a noncommittal sound.

"Anyway, would you tell him bye from me?"

"I will," Richard replied, trying desperately to figure out if this was some kind of threat. A way for Teresi of saying that he was onto the enhanced, maybe?

Teresi nodded and made his way back to the chick.

The temptation to discreetly pry open the envelope and have a peek inside was almost overwhelming. Eddie suggested flushing the letter out into the vacuum of space or burning it, and Richard did consider it. But he had no idea if Lieutenant Teresi had divulged the full contents of the Colonel's original message. It might specifically have told the recipient to report back via the same means. Or it might simply be standard procedure between them. Richard had never been a deep cover agent, and neither had he worked for Dietrich... except he kind of did now.

In any case, Richard kept the letter, all the way back to Stonehenge, in the chick as Eddie ferried him and Spencer back to the station proper. It was there when Eddie went back to the *Colibri* to pick up the passenger for the second trip. And when Dietrich's second in command, Captain Najjar, met him to take Spencer into custody and told Richard to go on to the Colonel's office.

It was still there when Richard sat down in the chair across from Dietrich and accepted another damn cup of green tea.

"I hope your injury is not serious," Dietrich said.

Richard knew better than to look surprised that they noticed. Medsys had informed him that his kinetic bullet wound was healing fine, but he was wearing a bandage under his sleeve, and his movements were more careful and stiff than usually. "It's not," Richard replied.

"May I ask what happened?"

"Yes," Richard said. "One of Spencer's people shot me with a kinetic projectile. I can't recommend it."

Dietrich winced in sympathy. "I am intimately familiar with the experience. Are you in need of any medical help?"

"No, I'm fine," Richard said, deciding that if the letter he was carrying elicited any unpleasant reactions from the Colonel, he could still change his mind and suddenly need immediate medical assistance as a diversion.

"Good. You... wouldn't happen to have kept the projectile, would you?" the Colonel asked.

"I figured you might ask," Richard said and fished the small lump of metal out of his pocket. He had cleaned it, but there wouldn't be any of the shooter's DNA on it, anyway. There also wasn't any marks on it, which meant that the weapon that had fired it might very well be illegal. He wouldn't get anything out of trying to trace it, though, so the Force might as well have it. "I also have a letter for you," he added.

Dietrich nodded, after flashing him a brief smile. "I expected as much."

"And," Richard continued, retrieving a small vial, too, "I have this as well."

"That looks remarkably like a blood sample," Dietrich said.

"Yes, from my pilot. Spencer's people captured her for a period of time during the mission. They did a pharmaceutically assisted interrogation."

Dietrich's eyes flicked from the vial in his hand to Richard's face. "I see," they said. "Is she in need of help?"

"She's a bit embarrassed, but her ego can take it," Richard said. He was a little surprised at the offer, really. But people reacted differently to aletheia, mentally and physically. Unlike Richard, Dietrich themself no doubt had failsafe, but obviously that wasn't something Eddie would even know existed.

"Good," the Colonel said. "Shall I take those off your hands?" They nodded at the two pieces of evidence.

"You'd better have this first," Richard insisted, holding out the envelope.

Dietrich took it and peeled off the adhesive strip without a word. They unfolded the piece of paper inside. Richard watched them for reactions as they skimmed the page. Nothing. Of course. They were better than that.

"I see you had the pleasure of meeting Lieutenant Teresi," they finally said.

"Yes." The palms of Richard's hands were starting to feel sweaty. It wasn't as if he was fiercely loyal to O'Connor. Besides, by now, O'Connor was probably already boarding another ship to get off Stonehenge. The problem was that Richard had lied. He wasn't entirely sure what the legal ramifications might be. He could always claim ignorance. But even if that should officially hold, Colonel Dietrich would never trust him with a job again.

"Now, as for the evidence material..."

"How much are they worth to you?" Richard asked.

Dietrich did not entirely manage to avoid looking surprised. "Not that much. They would indeed make a few things easier, but I have Spencer," they said.

"I see," Richard said, still holding the two items.

"Captain Hart," the Colonel said, not unamused, "are you trying to bribe me?"

Oh yes. That he was. "Of course not," he said. "I just recall you saying that this wasn't a job for you. That I wouldn't be doing anything for you that I wouldn't do for myself. Now, I personally wouldn't have kept the projectile as a memento, and nor would I have any use for a blood sample from my pilot... These things are for your benefit."

Micah Dietrich studied him over their steepled fingertips. Then they lowered their hands. "All right. As a token of appreciation, I will pay you for them. The amount is not for negotiation, but it should cover some of your expenses."

"Much obliged," Richard said and put the bullet and the vial on the shiny surface of the Colonel's desk. There definitely had been some unforeseen expenses. Richard knew Eddie usually asked him to pay for all sorts of small things for fun or to annoy him, but after her ordeal, he was going to get her a brand new patch instead of getting the old one repaired. And he might get Alannah a replacement for the artifact on her wrist too, if he could afford it. "I don't suppose you need me for anything else, then?"

"Not at this time, no," Dietrich said. "I am happy our interests coincided so well." They stood up and offered Richard their left hand.

"It was my pleasure," Richard said, shaking it. Although pleasure didn't really describe his feelings about the whole matter. At least there was one less person on the loose who wanted him dead.

As he was making his way toward the docks to rendezvous with Eddie, his patch informed him of a unit transfer. It was, surprisingly, more than the promised token of appreciation. Richard definitely could get his crew new patches now. He was, however, not at all surprised that it was another transfer labeled as "janitorial services". Hopefully, Eddie would never start looking into the finances of *Colibri* Investigations. He would never hear the end of it if she did.

While I stand by my claim that humanity as a whole is united in our day and age, it is also true that we will probably never reach åayu levels of harmony. Is it because we are mammals? Because we are omnivorous predators? Because our species grew up too quickly in some ways, and not quickly enough in others? Because our lifespan isn't long enough to grant us great wisdom? I don't know. I don't think anyone can know, really.

Bits of humanity will probably always attempt to break away from or revolutionize the rest. Sometimes these factions are right. Sometimes they are wrong. And often it's hard to say who is right or wrong, even in retrospect. There is crime, and there is disagreement. Humans are not unique in that among the sentient species in our galaxy.

So yes, humanity still has internal issues. But we have come a long way, haven't we? We do not wage mindless war on each other or try to conquer the homes of other species. And if there is one thing that traveling between the stars has taught me, it is that there is kindness to be found. Companionship. Camaraderie. Compassion. Sometimes, you have to search long and hard for it. Sometimes, it comes from strange and unexpected quarters. But it is there.

— Alannah Jackson, *The Human Legacy*

17
AFTERMATH

If Eddie had to rank every drug she had ever experienced, and there was rather a lot if she was honest, aletheia came in on the absolute last place. Ah, no, she corrected herself. That was actually reserved for that absolutely disgusting draever thing... Yuck. Anyway, aletheia landed on the place right above that. She was still feeling slightly queasy, despite the hyper and the anti-nausea medication medbay had advised. Worse than that, she had some toe-curling memories of the crap she'd said under the influence of aletheia. But all that didn't really matter. The important thing was that the not-job was done. They'd gotten the bitch who wanted Richard dead. And Richard was meeting with his secretive Colonel right now.

All that was left for Eddie to do was picking up Kierran from the *Colibri* and getting him to Stonehenge proper. They had decided it was better than bringing him on the first trip with Richard and Spencer.

Kierran was waiting for her when she landed. The airlocks had barely closed before he stood in the nest.

"Get in and let's get this over with," Eddie told him. At least Richard had dealt with the financial side of things before leaving.

Kierran nodded. He didn't have any luggage. He took the seat next to her in the chick without a word.

Eddie shot him a look as she turned the chick around and approached the outer airlock again. He was looking as blank as always. Blank and sinister, which shouldn't be possible, but clearly it was.

"So," Eddie began as she piloted them into the lane that would bring them to the station's docks. "I guess I owe you thanks."

A muscle in Kierran's jaw moved.

"For getting me out of there and all that," she continued.

Kierran gave a shake of his head that was so subtle it was barely noticeable, and for a moment, Eddie thought he wasn't going to even reply. "Just doing my job," he then said.

Eddie shrugged. It was true, in a way. But according to Richard, Kierran had volunteered to do it, and even though he probably only did to get the job over with so he could get back to whatever it was that he was going back to, he had saved her ass. "Still. Thank you," she said. There. Done.

Kierran nodded.

"You know," Eddie added, not entirely sure why she bothered, "you did a good job. You're not as bad as all that."

Kierran nodded again, his gaze focused on the docks ahead.

Eddie wondered if he didn't care, or if he was just extremely awkward with compliments. If it was the latter, she could relate. "So yeah. I appreciate the help. That's all." She swallowed and scratched the back of her head. "Look, I'm not going to apologize for saying I like Julien better than you."

This time, an actual expression stole over Kierran's features for a second. "I'm not expecting you to," he said.

"Good. Because I'm not," she concluded.

Ahead of them, the docks were growing bigger. It would only take them a couple of minutes to get there, and then Kierran would be out of Eddie's life. Good riddance. All she had to do was stand this awkward silence for a few more minutes... "So, what are you going to do now?" she asked because apparently she couldn't keep her big mouth shut.

A small, vertical crease appeared between Kierran's eyebrows.

"Are you going to keep killing people?" Eddie pursued the matter.

"I—" He hesitated. Fell silent.

"Because it's fucked up, you know. Pretty much the actual worst. And... you're better than that. It's never to late to change your path," Eddie said. Sure, she'd never murdered people, but she'd changed hers. Richard had picked up the pieces of his life and started something new. Even the least dysfunctional member of the *Colibri* family, Alannah, had done something pretty crappy and then changed direction.

Kierran was quiet for a moment longer. Eddie was beginning to regret she'd said anything. She honestly didn't know why she had. He wasn't anything to her. Just a perpetually pissed off guy who made his living killing for units. Just a guy she'd been told to babysit on a job. Just a guy who had rescued her because he stood to gain from it. She supposed she could actually turn him in to the authorities now. Give them an anonymous tip that the man who tried to kill Richard Hart was on Stonehenge. Send them a quick still of his face after he got out of the chick. Making sure there was one less hitman out there. Richard's code of honor or whatever it was be damned. He'd never even know she had—

"Thank you," Kierran O'Connor said.

Eddie blinked. Managed to get her expression back under control. "I didn't know you were even capable of those words," she snorted.

Kierran exhaled. It sounded remarkably like a sigh. "If it makes you feel better—"

"This isn't about me feeling good or bad," Eddie snapped. "It's about right and wrong. I'm no saint here, no one is, but..."

"Do you want to know or not?" Kierran almost sounded irritated.

"Okay, sure. Tell me. But do it quick. I want to get this little taxi gig over with."

"I am not going back to being an assassin," he said. "I no longer have a reason to."

"You had a reason before? Apart from making a bunch of quick units?" Eddie asked.

The corner of Kierran's mouth twitched. "I know a place where I can make the units I need, using the skills I have without killing anyone," he said. He didn't elaborate.

Eddie nodded. She eased the chick into the parking booth. "Okay. Good," she said.

"Will you..." He swallowed. "Will you tell Alannah that?"

"Say the magic word."

"The magic..?"

Eddie shook her head. "It's starts with P and ends with lease, you freak."

"Will you *please* tell Alannah?" he said, making it sound more sarcastic than even Eddie believed herself capable of, which was quite a feat.

"Yeah. I will," she said. Not to be nice to him, but because it would make Alannah happy to know. She was too damn kind to everybody, stray super soldier assassins included.

Kierran nodded. Apparently he had used up his meager stash of thanks.

The hatch of the chick opened. "Okay," Eddie said. "That's it. You're free."

Kierran stood up. He looked at her and nodded again. "Good bye," he said.

"Bye, bye," Eddie replied with a little wave of her hand that she intended to look nonchalant, but which didn't hit the mark exactly.

She watched him on the view screen as he walked away from the chick. He didn't look back even once. Good fucking riddance. "See you never, Kierran O'Connor," Eddie muttered to herself.

She sighed. Rolled her shoulders to get some of the tension out of them. She hoped Richard would be back from his meeting with the Colonel soon. She had done more than enough waiting around on Stonehenge Station to last her a lifetime.

Acknowledgements

You have now reached the book equivalent of a movie's credits. This is, in other words, where I get to thank a bunch of awesome people who made Assassins and Olympians a reality.

As always, I am grateful to Spaceboy Books in general for offering me a cabin on their amazing spaceship and letting me continue to share the stories I write and explore strange, new worlds with *Colibri Investigations*. Thank you to Nate Ragolia in particular for perfectly polishing off my prose and being so much better at coming up with snazzy back cover descriptions than I am.

My gratitude also to my wonderfully supportive family and friends who always have my back, and give me a space to rant about all those people living in the future/my mind.

Very special thanks to my team of beta and sensitivity readers for providing me with invaluable feedback, asking all the right questions, and loving the *Colibri* family. Also thank you to my Patreon supporters Gabe Clark, Ryan Watt, Skjalm, ZombiEdward and more. Your support means a lot to me!

Naturally, no acknowledgments are complete without my love and scritches to my dear feline friends who keep me company and purr everything better (and occasionally nap on my keyboard or block my view of the screen, but that's part of their charm).

And thank you! I hope you've enjoyed this *Colibri Investigations* novella, and that you will join the crew for another adventure soon.

Richard handed over the two small bags in a way that suggested he might as well have wrapped up the contents in nice paper and put ribbons on them.

"What is this?" Alannah asked, resisting the urge to peer into the bag just yet.

"Is it a pony?" Eddie said.

"Yes," Richard replied, deadpan as ever. "I got a toy pony for each of you. Go on, have a look."

Alannah took out a rectangular box with a familiar logo on it and opened it with due reverence. It was a brand new, state-of-the-art patch. The wristband and casing were an iridescent turquoise, and it was so thin and light that she would hardly feel it on her wrist. She had been drooling over this very model for weeks. "You shouldn't have!"

"Yeah, he should," Eddie said, inspecting her own new patch, the same model in black. She was smiling and there was no real bite in her tone. "Thank you, Richard. This is exactly the model I've been looking at!"

"Thank you," Alannah said and pulled Richard into a hug.

Richard grinned. "You're welcome. I owed Eddie a new one after she trampled hers in the line of duty. And yours was an ancient relic. So I—" His own patch interrupted with a chime. He looked at it, and his expression changed. "You two have fun with those, and I'll go and look at this message," he said.

"Trouble? A new job?" Eddie asked.

"I'm not sure," he said. "It's from an old friend I haven't talked to for quite a while."

About the Author

Marie Howalt grew up near Copenhagen in Denmark, Scandinavia and decided to become a writer at the age of 11 when the local library failed to deliver an acceptable amount of science fiction and fantasy.

Having graduated with a master's degree in religion and English studies with a primary focus on speculative literature, Marie wrote as a hobby and worked as a teacher and a translator between English and Danish before changing lanes in life due to chronic illness (post concussion syndrome).

Fast-forward to the present, and you will find Marie writing as much as physically possible. The tales are longer and more complex than the childhood fantasies, but they still take place in the far future or other worlds.

When not writing (or bribing imaginary people to share their stories), Marie is dedicated to being a cat perch, but also enjoys reading and listening to audiobooks as well as drawing, making videos, and collecting and restoring antique fountain pens. Sometimes, you can find Marie pushing art supplies, stationary and fancy pens in one of Copenhagen's oldest shops.

Marie's first traditionally published novel came out in 2019, and since then, there has been a steady flow of a new book every year (plus the odd short story). *Assassins and Olympians* is the second novella about *Colibri Investigations*, but the trusty little spaceship is already preparing to take flight again, so you won't have to wait for too long to join the crew on more adventures.

If you want to keep up with Marie's life and writing and get a healthy dose of cat pictures, please drop by Marie's Instagram profile @mhowalt. You can also get special perks and previews by newsletter or on Patreon via www.mhowalt.dk.

Other Works by Marie Howalt

Colibri Investigations
The Stellar Snow Job (2022)

The Moonless Trilogy
We Lost the Sky (2019)
Seeking Shelter (2020)
Heart of the Storm (2021)

A Moonless Novelette
Training Wheels (2021)

About the Publishing Team

Nate Ragolia is a lifelong lover of science fiction and its power to imagine worlds more hopeful and inclusive than the real one. His first book, *There You Feel Free*, was published by 1888's Black Hill Press in 2015. Spaceboy Books reissued it in 2021. He's also the author of *The Retroactivist* (2017). His most recent book, *One Person Can't Make a Difference* (2022), was featured on Tor.com's Can't Miss Indie Press Speculative Fiction list, and was translated into Italian for Ringworld Sci-Fi in 2023. He founded and edited *BONED*, a literary magazine, and also created two webcomics. Nate is also a husband and a dog dad.

Shaunn Grulkowski has been compared to Warren Ellis and Phillip K. Dick and was once described as what a baby conceived by Kurt Vonnegut and Margaret Atwood would turn out to be. He's at least the fifth best Slavic-Latino-American sci-fi writer in the Baltimore metro area. He's the author *Retcontinuum*, and the editor of *A Stalled Ox* and *The Goldfish* for 1888/Black Hill Press.